THE GOODBYE KISS

Massimo Carlotto

THE GOODBYE KISS

*Translated from the Italian
by Lawrence Venuti*

Europa
editions

Europa Editions
116 East 16th Street
12th floor
New York, N.Y. 10003
www.europaeditions.com
info@europaeditions.com

The author thanks Marcella D. R. Catignani and Valeria Pollino.

The translator thanks Clementina Liuzzi, Toby Olson
and, for the right sort of inspiration, Andrew Vachss.

Copyright © 2000 by Edizioni e/o
First Publication 2006 by Europa Editions

Translation by Lawrence Venuti
Original Title: *Arrivederci amore, ciao*

Carlotto, Massimo
The Goodbye Kiss

Library of Congress Cataloging in Publication Data is available
ISBN 1-933372-05-2

First Edition 2006

Book design by Emanuele Ragnisco
www.mekkanografici.com

PRINTED IN ITALY
Arti Grafiche La Moderna – Rome

THE GOODBYE KISS

Penal Code, Article 178:
Rehabilitation discharges additional penalties
as well as any other penal consequence of the sentence,
unless the law provides otherwise.

Penal Code, Article 179:
Rehabilitation is acknowledged when five years have elapsed
from the date on which the sentence is served,
or discharged by some other means,
and the convict has given positive
and consistent proof of good conduct.

Prologue

T HE ALLIGATOR WAS GENTLY BOBBING BELLY-UP. It'd been picked off because it started to get too close to the camp, and nobody wanted to lose an arm or a leg. The sweetish stink of decay mingled with the scent of the jungle. The first cabaña stood about a hundred meters from the clearing. The Italian was calmly chatting with Huberto. He felt my presence. He turned and grinned at me. I winked, and he resumed talking. I came up behind him, took a deep breath and shot him in the back of the neck. He collapsed on the grass. We grabbed him by the arms and legs and threw him beside the alligator. The reptile belly-up, the Italian face down. The water was so thick and stagnant that blood and scraps of brain sluggishly formed a spot no bigger than a saucer. Huberto took the gun from me, slipped it into his belt and with a nod signaled I should get back to the camp. I obeyed, even if I wanted to stay a little longer and stare at the body in the water. I didn't think it'd be so easy. I rested the barrel on his blond hair, careful not to touch his head, avoiding the risk that he might turn round and look me in the eye. Then I pulled the trigger. The shot was abrupt; it made the birds take off. I felt a slight recoil, and from the corner of my eye I saw the chamber of the semiautomatic slide back and load another round. My eyes, however, were focused on his neck. A little red hole. Perfect. The bullet exited the forehead, ripping open a ragged gash. Huberto watched him die without moving a muscle. He knew what was going down. The Italian had to be executed, and Huberto offered to lure him into the trap. For some time now he'd been a problem. At night he would get blind drunk and abuse the prisoners. The comandante called me into his tent the evening before. He was sitting on a cot, turning over a huge pistol in his hand.

"It's a nine caliber," he explained, "Chinese make. An exact copy of the Browning HP. The Chinese copy everything. They're careful, meticulous; if it weren't for the ideograms, you'd take it for the real thing. But the mechanism ain't worth shit. It jams at mid-clip. Perfect in appearance but weak inside . . . just like Chinese socialism."

I nodded, feigning interest. Comandante Cayetano was one of the original guerrilla cadres. And one of the few who survived. Now in his sixties, he wore a long, thin goatee just like Uncle Ho, and just like the Vietnamese leader he was long and thin. The son of a landowner who raised sugar cane, he chose to take up the cause of the poor and the Indios when he was young. Always stuck to the same line. Boring as hell, but macho. He definitely didn't call me over to jaw. He never did. He was never especially nice to me.

"Kill him," he said, handing me the pistol. "One shot should do it."

I nodded again. I didn't show any surprise, didn't even ask who I had to kill. It was obvious.

"Why me?" was the only question I allowed myself.

"Because you're Italian too." He spoke with a vicious tone that wouldn't stand any backtalk. "You came here together, and you're friends. It's better if this thing stays in the family."

I nodded again, and the next night I pulled the trigger. Nobody in the camp said a thing about what happened. They were all expecting it.

That was the sum total of my guerrilla experience, that double-crossing execution. Killing somebody who, like me, had decided to dedicate his life to the cause of a Central American people. To words. Fact is, we were two pricks filled with delusions of grandeur, who ran away from Italy and the stuck-up babes at the university, pursued by an arrest warrant for subversive activities, among a few other petty offenses. Not counting the bomb we planted in front of the offices of the Industrialists' Association. It killed a night watchman, some poor bastard about to retire. He spotted the bag, climbed off his bicycle and made the mistake of poking his nose into it. From the newspapers we learned he passed by every night. We simply didn't check beforehand; we were much too busy bragging at the bar about operations others had carried out. A girl I'd been with a couple weeks decided to come clean half an hour after her arrest, and she squealed on us. In a flash we crossed the French border. In Paris, a year later, when we heard we were sentenced to life in prison, we looked into each other's eyes and decided to play hero. Except the jungle wasn't the Latin Quarter or Bergamo, let alone Milano. And the enemy, if he captured you, didn't throw you in jail but skinned you alive from your ankles up. We arrived full of enthusiasm and healthy revolutionary fervor, but it took us a week to discover a guerrilla's life is utter hell. Luckily we always stayed behind the front lines. Unlike those silent Indios, we didn't have the balls to confront the dictatorship's rangers and their American instructors. The Indios never smiled. They lived and died with the same expression. My friend gradually went out of his mind. He started to drink and play weird games with the soldiers the Front captured in ambushes. I'd warned him certain failings weren't appreciated in those parts, but by then he'd stopped listening to anybody. During the day he moved like a robot, waiting for night.

I exploited the arrival of a Spanish TV crew to put some distance between myself and Comandante Cayetano, the danger of combat and the cause. I didn't give a damn anymore. A short fat-assed journalist had her eye on me. I led her to think she'd have a thrilling affair with one of the last fighters in the international brigades. After a few passionate nights, she requested and received the comandante's permission to have me assist her in the interviews. I escaped to Costa Rica, crossing the border on foot. I promised to join her in Madrid. But I needed a passport, and the thought of returning to Europe with a life sentence hanging over my head still seemed a pointless risk. I looked for work on beaches. European investors, particularly Italians, had begun building hotels on the most beautiful, pristine strips. There were no contractual obligations, no town-planning schemes; licenses were granted through a convenient system of bribes. An earthly paradise metamorphosed into a cement paradise. In addition to Italian, I spoke Spanish and managed quite well with French. I was hired as a bartender in a hotel owned by an Italian woman. She was loaded, in her forties, separated, no kids. A Milanese prone to affairs. The kind of woman who knows how to handle people. When I introduced myself, she gave me the once-over. She must've liked what she saw. But she wasn't stupid. She told me straight out I was clearly a terrorist on the run. One of the shitheads who'd destroyed her car to construct a barricade right in the center of Milano. She remembered the date. So did I. Three days of rage. The city stank of gasoline and tear gas and two deaths, Varalli and Zibecchi. I reeled off a lie that was pathetic but credible. She advised me not to act up; the Costa Rican police had no sympathy for political refugees. The place did seem like paradise to me, compared to the jungle, and for the first time after my escape I could entertain the idea of putting down roots. My fate was in my boss's hands, however, and slipping into her bed whenever it was vacant seemed the best method of keeping the situation under control. Her name was Elsa, and she wasn't bad-looking. Of course, women who were much more beautiful—and much younger—strolled the beaches. But I wasn't in a position to indulge in certain luxuries. She played hard to get and made me suck up to her for two months before I could kiss her. She doubted the sincerity of my love, as well as almost everything I told her. Lying to her was easy, and it gave me a kick: it let me construct a different identity. Like a fake passport. Except on the inside. It let me live long stretches without squaring accounts with my real life, which I began to hate. That frightened me. For too long my life was based on declarations of intent I never carried through. For lack of courage. And deep down I always knew it. But I had no problem lying to myself, not to mention the people at bars and meetings. They weren't all like me. Just the opposite. I formed part of that minority who found the movement a site of camaraderie and freedom. Things my family always denied me. If I imagined the price was life in prison and murdering a friend, I would've stayed put at home, stomaching my father's bullshit, my mother's failings, my sisters' bigotry.

Elsa preferred to screw in the morning, before getting breakfast for the guests. I always thought she preferred the morning because she didn't have to spend a lot of time having sex. She was always in a rush and totally without imagination. An orgasm, a kiss on the forehead, a cigarette. I first cheated on her two years later with another forty-year-old. A Florentine with her husband and sister-in-law in tow. On the pretext that her complexion was too fair and delicate, she spent most of her time perched on a barstool. Gin and tonic plus an endless desire to chatter. She was a little overweight, but she had a pretty face and a look in her eyes that said she was up to no good. She wasn't the only one; the others were all younger and more attractive. But I was drawn to the forty-year-olds. The thought of worming my way into their lives and toying with their weak spots made my head spin. I betrayed Elsa with no regrets. The others were a cinch. In those days I was little more than thirty and, like Elsa used to say, a handsome piece of ass. The bar was a strategic spot, and you didn't need a bunch of irresistible come-on lines. It was enough if your glances were just a bit shifty, if your smiles were polite and defenseless and if you were ready and willing to listen.

That's how I spent seven years. Almost without realizing it. Everything ended when Elsa unexpectedly came behind the bar and found me in the arms of a German broad. I don't remember her name, not even her face, but she was a very important pussy in my life. That fuck suddenly took away everything I had. The next morning I hightailed it from the hotel, bag in hand, and did a quick disappearing act. All through the night Elsa played the role of the betrayed benefactress; one way or another she was going to take revenge. A hell of a woman, but when she got pissed off, she lost her head. I had just enough time to steal the passport of a guest from Alicante who bore a faint resemblance to me. I dropped by a forger who used to hang out at the bar, had him substitute my photo and grabbed a direct flight to Paris. When I arrived at the airport, I thought of going to live in Mexico. It struck me as the most logical move. Then a trio of Air France stewardesses crossed my path. I stopped to check them out. And as I was admiring their asses, I decided to give my life a new twist. It was just a hunch, but enough to make me change my escape route despite the warrant that dogged my trail for more than ten years now. On the flight the hunch took shape, turned into a rock-solid decision, then into a well-defined plan, and when I sailed through customs, I hit the nearest pay phone. It wasn't easy to track down the person I was looking for, but in the end I got hold of him. He was surprised to hear from me after so long, and he wasted no time to ask if I was in a jam. I sighed and answered I had to see him on the double.

We met around lunchtime in a brasserie near the Gobelins

metro stop. I got there early and passed the time watching people come and go.

"Enrico, why d'you come back? What happened? Where's Luca?" he blurted, even before taking off his jacket. My immediate supervisor during the Parisian exile, he was using our noms de guerre. His real name was Gianni, but in the organization he was known as Sergio. He'd always been an intermediate cadre, carving out a career in France only because the bigwigs all got jailed in Italy. I looked him over. He had a peasant's face, and his hands were dirty with grease. Worked in some sort of factory. His life was waking at five in the morning to drag his class consciousness to the plant.

"Luca died a few years ago," I announced. "They caught him playing hide the salami with a captured official and laid him out."

"Are you shittin' me?"

I did nothing but stare at him.

"What about you?" he asked in a whisper.

"I fucking got fed up and came back."

Sergio bit into his sandwich, taking a moment to think. He chewed slowly and gulped down half a glass of red wine. To him I was nothing more than a pain in the ass, and it was his job to take care of the problem.

"What do you figure you'll do?"

The time had come to play my hand. "I'm heading back to Italy. I'm going to cooperate with the authorities and turn a new leaf."

He went white as a ghost. "You can't. We've already been wiped out by the turncoats. We shut down years ago, Enrico. The organization doesn't exist anymore, it's finito. The armed struggle is over."

"Then there's no problem," I cut him short.

"No, you know about too many comrades who were never ID'd. People who lead normal lives today. They don't deserve to end up in the slammer."

I shrugged. If I was in his shoes, I would've snarled and hissed a death threat. But he just winced. "What's happened to you?" he asked, running a hand over his face.

"I'm fed up with this shitty business," I shot back. "I don't have the slightest intention of spending the rest of my life in exile, every day risking jail for a stupid fucking night watchman and a few flyers."

Sergio tried one last appeal—to values and ideals. I waved him off. "Find a solution, Gianni," I said, shifting to his real name. "Otherwise I'll fuck over all the survivors. Your sister too, even if she didn't have shit to do with it. I'll add her name to the others. I'll say she brought me the explosive and the cops swallowed her story too fast."

I got up and left without even looking at him, leaving behind my beer and sandwich. The whole thing was a ball-buster. I didn't have much money, and that day I couldn't spend any more. Started knocking on doors, methodically, looking up people I knew during my first Parisian sojourn. I chose the ones who didn't have direct ties with the Italians. I knew there was nothing to fear from retired guerrillas, but you can never be too cautious. I had a fake passport and a conviction in Italy. A tip-off and they'd lock me up in La Santé with the Basques and the Muslims. A Uruguayan couple put me up, expatriates from a previous generation. He was an engineer, she a psychiatrist. The woman gave me a sympathetic ear. "One week," she finally said, jerking her thumb to make herself perfectly understood.

If you're up shit creek in a big European city and you're looking for a place to sleep with three squares a day, you need a system for tracking down a single woman. And if, like yours truly, you're not a bad-looking guy and have extensive experience with women past their prime, the chances for success increase appreciably. I plunked myself into an armchair and started poring over the personals in Saturday's *Libération*. Naturally, I had to focus on staunchly progressive neighbor-hoods where I could pass myself off as a combatant for Third World freedom. Rejecting women under forty and with chil-dren, I responded to about fifteen ads with voice mail boxes. Couldn't wait for the mail. A week later I brought my few rags to Régine's apartment near the Place de la Republique. Our first date happened at a photography exhibit in a private gallery. One of her friends was showing, and Régine was intrigued by the idea of meeting among a bunch of people she knew. I arrived determined to get somewhere. The other encounters were flops, and I swore not to be choosy, to turn on all my charm. But Régine was a real dog, and I had to force myself not to beat a retreat and vanish into the crowd on the Champs Elysées. Forty-seven, decent job, separated for ages, she had the face and body of a woman who'd let herself go and decided to give it up to lonely hearts. Somewhere along the way she registered it was too late to get back to even a vague facsimile of the woman she once was. At first she found it strange a man ten years her junior would date her. But she was horny, and the sex convinced her to take advantage of the opportunity. It was easier to make her believe she was living out some wonderful love affair than it was to screw her. But in the end she was the one who suggested we try shacking up, on the pretext that I needed a place and finding one in Paris wouldn't be a snap. She turned out to be an attentive lover, and my accommodations were definitely comfortable. Fact is, she was a petty woman, as ugly as her life. I couldn't believe that deep down she didn't suspect the mountain of lies I constant-ly unloaded on her. But loneliness made her vulnerable, if not simply deaf and blind. The little good sense she still had per-suaded her to keep her cash and jewelry under lock and key.

This agony lasted a couple months. Finally Sergio found a remedy. He arranged to meet me in the same brasserie as before. I found him already seated, staring intently at a quarter liter of red wine. He looked like some caricature of a tavern scene. Maybe he was dreaming of the one near his home in Italy, where he'd spend some time after work, rinsing the taste of the foundry from his mouth and talking politics, cursing the owners and the party leaders who betrayed the cause.

I sat down without saying hello. "So what's up?"

"We've conferred and decided to make you a proposition," he began. "Your conviction is a done deal, and the only hope of getting it thrown out is a retrial. We've convinced a comrade with a life sentence to confess to your role in the bombing. He'll say his conscience got to him, he was with Luca that day, and he'll provide some credible details. The lawyers say it should work. But you have to get used to the idea of doing some time."

"How much?"

"Two, three years, however long it takes to get through the courts. And then to make the conscience thing believable the comrade has to confess once you've turned yourself in. They'll also pin some related crimes on you, but you'll pay for those while you're awaiting retrial."

This isn't what I wanted. I lit a cigarette. "It's too much," I hissed.

Sergio shook his head. "Even if you cooperate and spill everything, they'll make you do some time. The lawyers say this is the best deal going on the bad rep market."

"Don't push me," I said calmly. "I'm resigning from the firm, and I'm just negotiating the settlement."

I ordered a beer and took a drag on my cigarette, weighing the proposition. "OK. I'll turn myself in at the border."

Sergio heaved a sigh of relief. From his pocket he took out a notebook and a pen. "Write down what you remember about that night, details especially. The confession has to be precise."

While I was writing, he asked me if I wanted to know what my old friends and comrades said about my sellout.

I smiled. "I already know. I know them inside out. They called me a piece of shit and made noise about getting revenge: a shot in the head, or an axe, just like Trotsky. A lot of hot air. The same old story."

"Don't you even want to know which comrade is going to pay for your crime?"

"No. I'll read about it in the newspapers. Besides, if he's doing it, he doesn't have a choice. Among the names I could finger I bet there's somebody who's dear to his heart."

I closed the book and threw some cash on the table.

"You really deserve to die." He was serious.

"Don't be pathetic." I left, certain I'd never see him again.

A couple weeks later I forced open Régine's desk drawer with a screwdriver, took her cash and jewelry and exited her life forever. The next day I'd surrender to the Italian police, and I planned to have a little fun before going to jail. I unloaded the jewelry on an Algerian fence from Barbès for some chump change. From the Gare de Lyon I took the train to Nice. I picked a deluxe hotel, a high-priced whore and a fine restaurant. When I woke the next morning, my pockets were empty. Thumbed it to the border.

Before taking me to San Vittore, the cops made a stop at the headquarters of the Digos in Milano, the division of general investigations and special operations. Also known as the anti-terrorist squad. They locked me in a room used for interrogations. Cigarette butts were heaped on the floor; blood and coffee spattered the pale green walls. The bulls liked to throw coffee at suspects, paper cups filled with disgusting shit, just to show they were pissed off and didn't drink what they tried to palm off on you. I felt calm, all things considered. I'd surrendered, delivering myself into the hands of the law. They couldn't break my balls any more than this. Some cop came in with a file under his arm. He was tall, huge, with a face like a pig. He wore a swanky suit. I lowered my eyes to his shoes. Unmistakably pricey. Either he came from money or was on the take. I opted for the second hypothesis and relaxed.

He slammed the file on the table and sat down. "My name is Ferruccio Anedda, and I am a very important person."

I limited myself to a slavish nod. Didn't want any trouble. Cops like to have the situation under control.

"Who made you come back from Central America?" he asked, letting me know straight off they had much more information than I imagined.

"I just got out. I want to pay my debt to society—"

He kicked me under the table. "We know everything. You blackmailed those shits who're holed up in Paris, and you're planning to act out a little farce for the judges."

I stared at him, amazed. "You've got an informer in Paris?"

He cocked his head. "Only one?" he said ironically.

"What do you want?"

"Here's what I would like," he said, satisfied. Then he changed his tone: "We want the names of everybody who has never been identified. Especially the collaborators. Otherwise, at the proper moment, I'll have a little chat with the chief justice and you'll pay in full for the night watchman."

"The lawyers say it isn't in my interest to play turncoat." I took a chance, putting out a feeler to see if there was any room for negotiation.

"You're useless to us as a turncoat. We're not planning to scrape the bottom of the barrel. The organization has been fucked for years. We simply put them under surveillance, so if somebody gets the crazy idea to jump-start the wreck, we're on to them immediately and save ourselves a ton of work."

"What's in it for me, apart from getting off for the night watchman?"

"Doesn't avoiding a life sentence seem like enough to you?"

I spread my arms. "I can be very helpful."

The bull snorted. "We can help *you* and make your stay in jail more comfortable."

I lit a cigarette and started ransacking my memory. An hour later the organization was liquidated definitively. I could've kept on supplying information I gathered on other groups over the years, but at this point I felt it'd be a total waste. Might come in handy later. I've always had a good ear, and in Italy the militant underworld always distinguished itself by being off-hand about security precautions. They talked in no uncertain terms about safeguarding the organization, but in practice they honored none of it, showing a downright weakness for shooting off their mouths and telling secrets.

I got to the prison before nightfall. They brought me straight to the registration office, and Anedda whispered something into a sergeant's ear. The officer turned towards me and winked. The cop had passed on the orders. I'd have to squeal for the prison guards too. A corporal took me by the arm and led me to a counter where he opened a register that looked like something out of the nineteenth century.

"Surname?"

"Pellegrini."

"First name?"

"Giorgio."

"Date and place of birth?"

"May 8th 1957, Bergamo."

The guard stopped writing. "May 8th," he repeated. Then he turned to the others: "This guy was born on the same day Gilles Villeneuve died."

"I didn't know. When did it happen?"

The corporal glared me in shock. "Ten years ago, in 1982. The greatest tragedy in the history of car racing." He pointed towards a wall where a little altar was set up with the photo of the Formula One driver between Ferrari pennants. Then he pointed his finger in my face. "In this office everybody supports Milan and Ferrari. Understood?"

At San Vittore I settled in right away. Getting by without a scrape wasn't hard; you just had to respect the unwritten rules and fuck all the rest. They made me work as a janitor. I had to sweep the corridor in my block and keep my eyes peeled, especially with the foreigners. Every so often they called me into a little room near the guard station and asked me for information about a few jailbirds. I soon learned the trick was to badmouth the ones who weren't popular in the head office, even if they hadn't done a thing. Sometimes I just cooked up tales; other times I reported what I'd seen. Now and then Anedda showed up to get more details or explanations. If I needed something, I bargained on the remuneration, and when all was said and done, the bull was openhanded. In time he even got into the habit of bringing me a bottle of whiskey. He was my only visitor. My family never came to see me. They disowned me when I skipped to Paris. My father's curses chased me down the stairs of our house, and I ran like a shot, never turning back. In the beginning I was really racked, but fate took me a good ways off, and at this point I almost never thought about it.

I was on friendly terms with the die-hard who took the rap for the night watchman's murder. His name was Giuseppe. One of those guys who regretted nothing because he remained a communist and a revolutionary. He worked for Dalmine, the machine factory, like his father and grandfather. Started out gung-ho for the union and the party, photos of Lenin, Togliatti and Berlinguer on the kitchen wall. Then he took a different path and went underground. He was rousted by a stoolie, but when he opened his own mouth, he said only—in dialect, pure Bergamasco—that he was a political prisoner.

In Paris they must've broken open the piggy bank. They

bought me a lawyer who was once a militant in Soccorso Rosso but then established a solid career, joining a new center-right political party. He told me he took on the case because retrials were all the rage, they generated enormous publicity, and in my particular situation there were real prospects for success. He also showed himself capable of dealing with the press, since dailies and magazines were buzzing around me. Meanwhile days slipped by, and I began to mull over my future. So I wouldn't leave with empty pockets I ran a little traffic covered up by some guards. For one stretch I took a Brazilian trans-vestite under my protection. On odd-numbered days, when it was our turn in the shower, I organized a series of tricks, not more than five at a time to avoid attracting attention. One car-ton of Marlboros for a blowjob, two for a fuck. I gave him ten percent and the assurance that nobody would slash his face. The guards would call on him in his cell at four in the morn-ing. But that wasn't any of my business. Nor was there any-thing to be gained from it. The prison staff never paid. At that time I also made a slew of interesting acquaintances. Professionals of every criminal persuasion offered me their friendship. In the past, a turncoat, especially somebody sus-pected of being in cahoots with the cops, would've been knifed as soon as he stuck his nose out of his cell. But nowadays even prisons aren't what they used to be.

The judicial process took its course. Slow but unstoppable. The Court of Cassation granted the retrial and sent the records to the appellate division of the Court of Assizes in Milano. At the trial, Giuseppe took pains to avoid looking me in the face. When the lawyer addressed the court, he explained Giuseppe's attitude as shame for making me lead the life of a fugitive. Anybody could've seen it was merely disgust. But by then the 1970s was stale news around the court house. The judges' deliberations lasted a couple hours, just long enough to write the decision. I was acquitted. Still had to serve another couple months for belonging to an armed group, but finally I'd be released from the nightmare. It started many years ago, when Sergio met me in a bar on the outskirts and proposed I join the organization. Secret, communist, militant.

One morning they told me to turn in my mattress, sheets and mess tin at the storeroom. I'd just turned thirty-eight. At the exit I found Anedda.

"Remember you belong to the Milanese Digos," he barked.

"I've retired," I answered in a huff.

The bull slammed me against the wall. "You owe me a shit-load of favors. And don't ever forget somebody else is doing your time."

I pried myself loose from his grip and set off along the perimeter wall. I spied freedom on the other side of the street, but I still didn't feel ready to go for it. When I reached the tower, I crossed over.

FLORA

THE NOSTALGIA I FELT FOR MY COUNTRY and my once carefree life crystallized into a childhood memory. My paternal grandparents lived just outside Bergamo, and when they came to visit me and my sisters, they always brought us a gift, a box of Otello Dufour, the best bonbons in the world. I'd grab a handful of those goodies and retreat to my room or the garden with an adventure novel by Emilio Salgari, unwrapping one after another, laying it delicately on my tongue and letting it slowly melt away. During the years when I was either on the lam or behind bars, my most private and painful memories were always capped by the desire for a chocolate liqueur-filled bonbon. When you're in prison, you're thinking all the time about the first thing you'll do when you're set free. My desire was stamped Dufour. I bolted into the first pasticceria I came across and bought an entire box. But as soon as I unwrapped one, I realized something wasn't right. Its shape was round, not oval, and it wasn't made of smooth chocolate as dark as mystery, but lighter and dotted with bits of hazelnut. I slipped it into my mouth—and almost gagged when it didn't taste anything like my childhood Otello. I felt double-crossed, ready to start bawling. For years I dreamed of something that didn't exist anymore. I went back into the shop, and the owner clinched it: the Otello had been turned into a kind of chocolate-coated candy.

"The things people like today," he said with a shrug.

I tossed the box into a trash can. I'd been let down, and it worried me. If I just got out of prison and ran into such tough luck satisfying my first wish, my life from here on wasn't going to be a stroll in the park.

Milano had changed too. It was crawling with freeloading foreigners bent on picking Europe's bulging pockets. We were in the exact same situation. I was alone, and after so many years away I felt like I knew Italy even less than they did. I took shelter in a religious community that offered assistance to ex-cons. Had a long heart-to-heart with a priest, a tough Abruzzese in the Mercedari order who hung around prisons too long to listen to any bullshit. I leveled with him. "I'm scared stiff. I don't know how to deal with this world; it's not what I was used to."

He sized me up. "I've kept my eye on you these past few years. You're a bad egg. As bad as they come." Then he clapped me on the knee a couple times. "But everybody deserves a second chance. You can stay here a little while, but don't dream of acting the way you did in San Vittore."

I thanked him, and as I walked away, he added: "Don't bother pretending you're a believer. It isn't necessary here."

The money I saved in prison was slipping through my fingers, and what I earned in the community, assembling shoe racks for a company that specialized in TV sales, wasn't even enough for cigarettes. Every time I went out I came back more broke. A meal in a trattoria to forget the slop cooked by a couple of former junkies. A toss with a streetwalker to make up for what prison forced me to do without. That was all I could allow myself. I'd go to the centro and spend hours eyeing the people and cars. A ton of cash was floating around, and most-ly everybody was oozing confidence. I felt out of place. Tried to hook up with an elegant forty-something. Milano was full of women like Régine, but much prettier and much more screwable. Dieting, working out at the gym, going to the hairdressers. I got off on their need to be constantly competitive in terms of beauty and sensuality. But there was no way they'd notice me. My face told my story: I was a marginal, an outcast. I looked for work, but it dawned on me if I took that approach, I'd be fucked for eternity. I'd stay a bum. My plans for the future went no further than mere subsistence, observing the world from the back of a fast-food restaurant, my hair rank with grease. Money. I needed money to lift myself from the dung heap I was stuck in. Then I'd establish a respectable position and stroll through the centro dressed to the nines, flaunting the worry-free face of a winner. And I wouldn't make the same mistake as everybody I met in San Vittore: try to make money, but stay a fucking hood. If you took that route, the only sure prospect was jail. Risking another court date made sense only if the cash was a means of elevating yourself socially. When I was living with my family, before getting involved with the movement and letting them fuck with my brain, I belonged to middle-class Bergamo. Thinking back on how I sneered at that scene made me feel like banging my head against a wall.

I started to lose hope fast. Even being a criminal wasn't easy. The city was armor-plated, and any action you might horn in on was already under the control of gangs from Eastern Europe, North Africa or the Far East. The priest made me take a job in a bar. It turned out to be my lucky break. One morning I served coffee to an old acquaintance from San Vittore. A guy from Bari who got time off for ratting on a boss in the Pugliese mafia, the *Sacra Corona Unita*.

"How's it going?" I asked him, checking out his smart suit.

"Aces with me," he answered, eyeing in turn my plastic wristwatch. "But you . . . what are you doing working a counter? You're wasted here. You sick? A big dude like you could be earning his living in a more dignified way, no?"

His tone was sarcastic. I wanted to slash his face with the

knife I used for peeling lemons. I smiled instead. "I'm looking for the right opportunity."

He drank his coffee and waved me over. "I've set up a business in Veneto, near Treviso," he explained. "Lap dancing, a joint where girls dance topless and guys drool and slip cash down their knickers. I need somebody I can trust to keep an eye on the clientele. You interested?"

"Does it pay?"

He showed me a row of nicotine-stained teeth. "Very well. I kid you not."

"Then I'm interested." I put some umph into it.

He handed me a card with the details about the place. It was called Blue Skies—in English. Not what I'd call a stroke of genius. "Show up tomorrow night."

When he was opening the door to leave, he had an afterthought and turned back. "I know you're an informer," he said under his breath. "So am I. I just want to be up front so we don't step on each other's toes."

Blue Skies was formerly a disco. Situated in the middle of the deserted countryside, it guaranteed a fair amount of discretion to its clientele. It was a cash cow, and like the owner said, a dozen foreign broads danced, shaking their asses at the customers who'd stretch out an arm to slide banknotes into their G-strings. Not every girl was a knockout. Faces didn't count for much. The job qualifications were ranked in the following order: tits, legs, height, ass.

For a hundred euros a day, I handled the customers who requested a private session. A guy would come to me, point out a dancer, and when she was free, I'd send her over to a private booth to perform exclusively for him. Every so often I managed to pull in some tips, and the salary wasn't bad. But this line of work wasn't going to get me very far. The most I could expect was to own another topless joint. Just like the

Barese, who sported gold around his neck and wrists and kept the nails on his pinkies about four centimeters long. A hood who commanded respect. But he wasn't my shining example. Still, I liked Veneto. It was on the fringes, and everybody had a chance to make it. All you needed was a little imagination, the drive to act and zero fear about sticking it up the next guy's asshole. First on the list was the State and its fucking taxes. I knew guys who used to go around in rags, then they found the right racket, and now they were sliding their asses into the leather seat of a Mercedes, dropping five hundred a night on the girls.

After three months of the same old tune, I decided to rip off the Barese. It'd be risky because he was sharp as a tack, nothing got by him, and he trusted nobody—the essentials for dodging any loss of respect. To make dead sure you got the message, he appeared in public with his two Romanian gorillas, ex-miners who were beefy and cruel. Used to work for Miron Cosma, the boss who led his sooty-faced thugs to Bucharest to teach a lesson to the rebellious students. Instead of heading back to dig coal, they crossed the border to make a pile.

Convinced I was sharper than the Barese, I started shaving off the take from the private sessions. The first move was to break it to the girls, who gave me a percentage. Ten percent from every customer. Which meant another hundred and fifty, two hundred every night. Some nights were really busy, and the dancers did more than twenty sessions. Since I was the one who kept track of the services and the take, I occasionally "forgot" to cue a customer and pocketed his money. During weekends I managed to earn another five hundred a night.

One Saturday, just before closing time, a Slovenian chick with a nasty tongue signaled me to follow her into the dressing room where she made a scene, yelling she wanted her money or she'd spill everything to the owner. You can bet I was primed for a situation like this, and I came right back at her. I clipped her hard in the pit of the stomach. Whores are used to getting slapped around, like the Romanians explained to me, and they can take it. She fell to the floor. I grabbed her by the hair, forced her to her knees and shoved my cock into her mouth. I felt her go slack, probably thinking she got off easy. I let her think it. All of a sudden I pulled her up and spun her around, smacking her against the wall; then I tore off her G-string and fucked her up the ass. She tried to get free, but I punched her in the kidneys. That made her settle down.

"Tell the other girls about our tête-à-tête," I said, zipping up my trousers. "And don't forget: anybody who doesn't play my game goes back home. I know the right cops. You understand?"

She lowered her head. I grabbed her by the chin. "But you don't have to worry. You I forgive, and I won't have you escorted to the border."

"I'm sorry, I didn't want to cause problems," she said in tears.

"Brava! A little education never hurts," I said, giving her a pat on the cheek. The bitch fell for it hook, line and sinker. Barely nineteen, she hadn't been here long. Dreamed of becoming a dancer in Las Vegas and getting her knickers stuffed with dollars. Thick as she was she'd never make it.

With the new cash flow I could afford to rent a house in town. Up till then I lived in a one-room flat carved out of the top floor of the club. It goes without saying I located the house through a customer who ran a real-estate agency. That's how things worked at the club. When somebody needed a favor, they turned to the right customer. In town they knew who we were, even the ones who never set foot inside Blue Skies and made out like they were moralists in public, looking down their noses at us. They acted the same way people did with brothels, like real holier-than-thou hicks. Even the widow Biasetto, the cleaning woman, didn't stop herself from bad-mouthing the place. But we had the customers by the balls. We knew everything about them because they confided more in the girls than in their parish priest. After I closed on the house, part of a two-family dwelling, and furnished it cheaply thanks to a lot of furniture dealers who appreciated the private sessions, I started hanging around town, shrugging off the looks I drew from people. I could've got myself a decent car, but that would make me more conspicuous, especially with the carabinieri, who stopped me every time we bumped into one another. When they checked my documents, I turned out to be a dangerous ex-terrorist, and they used it as an excuse to search my car and give me the third degree about the Barese's business. They were hoping to nab me with some of the cocaine that flooded the club, but I wasn't a dope. So I had to content myself with a used Panda. At the wheel of the compact I gave the impression of being the lowest gopher at Blue Skies. I consoled myself by dreaming of the pimpmobile I'd buy some day.

One winter afternoon, as I was strolling beneath the porticoes, I stopped to look into the window of a shoe store. It belonged to a dealer who had the twin vices of dancers and blow. At the cash register I spotted a gorgeous woman about forty. Blond, turned-up nose, fleshy lips, blue eyes. I shifted over to the next window to see her better. She wore a close-fitting black suit and shoes with the steepest heels. I went inside to try on a pair of moccasins I didn't need. Worked it so she'd have to help me. She had a faint net of wrinkles around her eyes and the no-nonsense look of a woman who made it the hard way. I learned her name was Flora. Flirted a little and bought the shoes. I came back over the next few days, and when her husband wasn't there, I took advantage of it and went inside to shoot the breeze with her. She was less and less nice. One morning she checked to make sure there were no customers and told me point-blank to cut out bothering her. She spoke in dialect and used expressions as tough as slaps. I grumbled a few words of apology and slipped out the door. Tried to forget about her, but day after day Flora became my obsession. I went to sleep and woke up thinking about her. One night I ran into her husband at the club. He wanted some coke on credit, and right then I saw how I'd get his wife into bed. I started to supply him with drugs and girls, assuring him he could pay at his convenience. He let the machine chew him up like a real idiot. Then one day I went to see him in his store. I waved him over. Flora was there too. I winked at her.

"Your account has hit ten thousand. Time to settle up."

He turned pale. "I don't have it. You've got to be patient."

"I can be as patient as you like," I lied, feigning sympathy. "The problem is the Barese. You know how he is, a fucking southerner, and when somebody doesn't pay, it's like a bug up his ass. You'll get a little visit from the Romanians, who'll break your arms and legs. This is the way it works."

"Help me, please," he whined, desperate.

"In a week the balance will double. You know how these things go. You're not a kid anymore."

"Help me. We're friends."

I made as if I was keeping an eye on the store. "Who's that looker?" I asked, pointing at Flora.

"She's my wife," he answered, surprised.

I grabbed his arm and squeezed it hard.

"Now you know how I can help you."

I loosened my grip and left.

He didn't show up that night. A few days later, as I was leaving the club at four in the morning, a car flashed its lights to catch my attention. I strolled over. It was Flora's Hyundai coupe. She rolled down the window.

"I'll follow you home," she said without feeling.

I showed her into the living room. She took off her fur. "Do you want to screw me here or in bed?" Her tone was disagreeable.

"Beat it," I hit back, irritated. "Tell your husband to come up with twenty grand by tomorrow or the Romanians'll show up. At the store. So the whole town'll know how he pissed away his money."

She raised her arms in a gesture of surrender.

The babe had to be tamed. I decided to lay it on thick by throwing her out of the house.

I left her in the cold for some twenty minutes. She didn't move. She just kept ringing the bell.

"Beat it," I repeated through the intercom.

"Let me in. Somebody might see me."

I pressed the buzzer and went over to the couch. When she came in, I patted the seat next to me. I caressed her face with the back of my hand, then slipped it under her short leather skirt and started fiddling with the elastic of her thigh-highs.

"You're decked out like a real slut," I snickered to insult her.

She lowered her face. "This is what I have to do to save the store and our reputations. Mine and my asshole husband's. Just how long does this thing have to go on?"

"Till your husband pays up. Minus the interest, of course. You pay that."

"On one condition: my husband mustn't set foot in that club ever again."

"It's a deal." I gave in, although in fact the thought had already crossed my mind. I couldn't risk letting the sap go around blabbing about the debt, wrecked on coke and alcohol. The owner would get wind of everything.

I moved close to kiss her.

She pushed me back. "No, no kissing."

Her rebuff turned me on even more. I forced her to look me in the eyes. "We make like two kids on their first date or the deal's off."

The thing with Flora fucked with my concentration. Whenever I thought about her, my cock got hard, and when I couldn't wait till nighttime, I showed up at the store during the lunch break, hung around till the salesgirls left, and banged her among the stacks of boxes in the back room.

Two Romanian dancers turned up at the club, but I didn't pay attention, charging them the usual percentage for the private sessions. It stands to reason they'd immediately go and tell the gorillas about it. At the end of the night the Barese came up to me, smiling, and asked me to join him in his office. The gorillas broke my left arm. The bone made a noise like a snapped branch. The pain was unbearable. I threw up on the carpet. Paid for my weakness by taking a punch in the fractured arm. Then they sat me in a chair in front of the owner.

"You devised an ingenious scheme, I must admit," he congratulated me as he examined the nails on his pinkies. "And intelligent people deserve respect. This is why I told the Romanians to rough you up just a little. The girls already get enough. You'll continue to collect the ten percent on every private session. But you'll put it in the cash box. The next time I catch you with your hand in the cookie jar you'll wind up dead and buried. The boys are very skillful at digging deep holes."

I looked at the gorillas. First they'd beat me to death, then get the shovels from the trunk of the car.

"All right, I'll straighten up," I promised, relieved the owner was in the dark about my blackmail of the shoe dealer. Otherwise I would've had to pay for it with the other arm. And kiss goodbye to Flora and the ten grand I still expected to pocket sooner or later.

The next night the dancers started to get uppity, giving me wise-ass looks, snickering behind my back. To restore order I had to make a scene in the dressing rooms and throw some jars of face cream against the wall.

I went back to earning a hundred a day, and the prospect of

going broke again drove me to sharpen my wits. Despite my fix-
ation on Flora. The broad loathed me. On no account would
she ever willingly go to bed with me. And this is exactly what
made the thing such a kick. I forced myself not to think about
her while I was working, and very soon I began to solve my
financial problems. The owner of a workshop that produced
fake Florentine lace asked me for a hand to sneak a group of
Bulgarian embroiderers into Italy. It was a snap, and I got paid
handsomely. The word spread. A couple stockjobbers had con-
tracts to sew jeans for a name brand advertised on TV, and they
needed some Chinese labor. It was a matter of driving a van
from Milano to Treviso; the envelope I made them give me in
advance contained a wad of two hundred euro notes. The
owner of a fishery had me poison a competitor's tanks. When I
emptied the cans, the water started to bubble, and the surface
was covered with stiff trout. I always did everything calmly, was
never afraid. All I thought about was the money.

Blue Skies was of course patronized by hoods. Italian and
foreign. But I never had anything to do with that element and
always confined myself to polite but formal relations. All the
same, I kept an eye on them and soon noticed how well honest
and criminal customers mixed together. The police had the
club under surveillance, but they too got a slice of the pie. The
Barese's philosophy was based on payoffs and informers.

I often helped with wrapping up deals. Particularly in the
insurance line: fires in warehouses, thefts of tractor-trailers,
stolen goods. Crimes or incidents of damage to non-existent
merchandise. Made my first real money by ruining a family
man who loved the dancers but was unlucky enough to be living on a tax inspector's salary. The first time he showed up with
a couple of local manufacturers. I'd already been tipped off so
I arranged a series of private sessions with the prettiest girls.
Right away it was obvious the dude went for a Dominican
chick, tall and slender. I organized a private performance for

him. Told the girl to give him some mouth action, and his two friends would pay her well. He quickly became a regular at the club. In the beginning he spent only what he could afford, and I worked overtime to convince him I could give credit at zero interest. "It's like buying a car on time," I told him with a smile. He finally gave in, and when the account got to be too big for his means, the two manufacturers sketched a plan that would take care of the debt by obliging him to close both eyes to their bookkeeping practices. Like Flora's husband, he let himself be fucked over. While I worked at Blue Skies, I saw so many like them. And yet the game was played with the cards on the table. Setting aside the ingénues and the idiots, I always thought these people couldn't wait to debase themselves. The scams with the dancers and the coke represented no more than opportunities to take the leap and enjoy life.

The club was a world apart that existed only by night and vanished by day. In time I started to fear it. If I kept working there, I'd be trapped forever. I'd confuse reality with the lie created by the dim lights and the dancers' heavily made-up faces. When I counted my little nest egg and saw it amounted to a cool thirty thousand, I thought the time had come to shift gears. But leaving the Barese wasn't easy. You couldn't just announce you quit. In his fucked way of thinking, so typical of a hood from southern Italy, that decision belonged to him alone, and for the time being I was still useful to him. While I was waiting for the right moment to end my contract with Blue Skies, the Romanians called on me one night. They needed to teach a lesson to four Albanians who bothered a few dancers in town. I tried to convince them not to get me involved in any punitive expedition, but I realized if I insisted too much, those two animals would've pounded me like a drum. We got into a stolen car. One of them handed me a pickaxe. The Albanians lived out in the country in an isolated house among frost-covered vines and soybean fields. The gorillas' plan was simple.

Smash open the door, raise hell on the way in and whack them right and left. For me fate reserved the only Albanian armed with a knife. I tried to bash in his head, but he avoided the blow, which caught him on the right knee. The pain made him pass out. One of the Romanians screamed at me to hit him in the face. I struck him three times in a rage. At home I had to throw out my blood-stained trousers. The incident got a short notice in the local newspapers. One of them died from a crushed skull. Maybe the guy I hit. Maybe not. The Albanians were scumbags; at the bar in town people celebrated with a round of prosecco.

One night after work I spotted Flora waiting for me outside my house, sitting in her car. I walked over, smiling. We didn't meet that day, and for a moment I kidded myself she really wanted to be with me. Instead she rolled down her window. She smiled at me like she never did before. Her black-gloved hand gave me an envelope.

"Here's the ten thousand. Count it if you want. We can finally say goodbye," she told me, satisfied.

I felt numb. I didn't want to give up this woman, the power I exerted over her body. "Flora—"

"Flora shit," she cut me off in a fit of anger. "Now get out of my life."

She started the engine and disappeared into the night. I knew I'd lost her forever. If I made a big deal about it, she'd go and complain to the Barese, and I'd wind up in deep shit. I went inside the house. With a knife I removed the bricks under the sink and added the money to my stash. Forty thousand. Now that was saying something.

The next day I took a stroll through the centro. When I passed by Flora's store, I didn't even glance in the window. I was again in pursuit of a lover, and I covered the area methodically, patiently. But nowhere did I find a woman as beautiful and sensual as her.

That night, after a slow, uneventful day, I left the place a little early. I went to a club in Jesolo where I heard a forty-something English entraîneuse was working. She was a letdown. Thin as a rail, flat chest. She had her clientele, but she wasn't my type. I bought her a drink. Forced myself to listen to some bullshit stories, then went home. Every once in a while the desire to see Flora came over me, but fear stopped me in my tracks. Only that. Otherwise I would've done something stupid just to be with her again.

I had a thing with the widow of a Milanese crime boss. After her husband died, murdered in a maximum-security prison, she lost power and money. She was now making do by working hotels. She played the role of the grande dame, refined, classy, specializing in bald traveling businessmen in their fifties with paunches and swollen wallets. It was me who hooked up with her, after watching her fail to snare the owner of a Val d'Aosta cheese factory. I suggested we have a drink.

"Don't I seem a little too mature to you?" she asked, surprised.

I looked her over. She must've been a very beautiful woman once. Now she was fifty, fighting against time and wrinkles so she wouldn't end up streetwalking at twenty euros a pop.

"Do you want to have a drink or go back to the cheesemaker?" I cut her short.

She was experienced but simpatica. She jabbered away, steering neatly between topics to avoid seeming like a gossip or a noseybody. With a few well-aimed questions I gathered she was going through a rough patch. That was exactly what I hoped to learn. I got off on the idea of how low she might sink for some real money, how much she'd humiliate herself. While she was telling me a couple stories about a trip to Vienna, I interrupted her. I leaned close to her ear and mentioned a figure. Then I asked if she felt like doing something for me. She pretended to be scandalized, but from the expression on her face I knew her response would be positive. I toyed with her dignity for a couple months. More than once she took the money in tears. One night she asked me how I could be so disgusting. At that point she left. Better that way. I was fed up too, and the whole business was costing me a lot of money. But her question set me thinking. She was right, I was disgusting, or to be more exact I was a bad egg, like the priest said. It caused me no shame. I was aware of it, but the fact is, wielding power over weak women helped me get by. Feel better. Survive. Deal with my past, the Barese's abuses, all the shit at the club. Finally it was a question of exchange value. Everything balanced out. Once upon a time I wasn't like this, but things I went through transformed my life. I changed. I felt like something inside me had snapped. Maybe some asshole psychoanalyst would've said prison had destroyed my sense of balance. The relation between the guards and convicts really wasn't so different from what I set up with Flora or the widow. Maybe it happened before, in Paris or the Central American jungle. But I didn't want to think about it too much. For me, San Vittore was a jumbled-up heap of fragmented sights, noises and smells. If I concentrated, I could probably put my memories back into some rational order. But I was afraid of going to pieces. Too little time had gone by. I could find some meaning in life and imagine a future only by constantly testing myself with extreme experiences. I liked being a bad egg. And I finally had a chance to become a winner.

Summer came. The work at the club was getting heavier, and I still hadn't found a way to cut myself loose without getting on the Barese's wrong side. One day the barman told me some guy was asking for me. I recognized him from behind. I'd seen him too many times walking down the corridor of block six, pushing the laundry cart. His name was Francesco Casu, alias Ciccio Formaggio: "Casu" in Sardinian means "formaggio"—cheese. But you'd only find him in Sardegna during the summer, visiting his grandparents. He hailed from Milano, where he was born. He'd also been mind-fucked by some militant and pulled off his silly stunts till they arrested him, giving him the chance to turn state's evidence. I didn't care much for the guy, thought him a loser. As I walked over to him, I hoped he hadn't come all this way to ask me for a job.

I got it wrong. He'd come to offer me a job. A robbery. The take: half a million euros. At least.

I looked him right in the eye. "Why me?"

He opened his arms. "Because I'm just the tip-off and don't know shit about how to organize a heist. You came to mind because of your experience with the Central American guerrillas. You can plan a military operation."

"How d'you learn about the job?"

"A security guard."

"They're the first to sing."

He lowered his voice. "I've thought about leaving him out when we split the cash. One more cut for the rest of us."

"Who else is in on it?"

"Apart from you, nobody."

"The target?"

"An armored truck in Varese. Every Saturday night, as punctual as a Swiss train, it comes to collect the week's receipts from a superstore. Two guards get out, open the night safe, pull out the bags and leave."

"The bit about the half a million . . . does it hold water?"

"Hell yes. I said *at least* half a million. According to the inside guy, it's never less than three quarters."

I drained my gin fizz, mulling over the proposition. The amount was worth the risk of going back to jail, especially if it didn't have to be split up too many ways. The guard would be the first to die, then Ciccio Formaggio. He was much too stupid to live with a secret that implicated me. I'd tie up any loose ends later.

"Before I decide, I want to see the place and the pick-up."
"Don't worry. I'll arrange it."

The following Saturday I was in the parking lot of a huge superstore, pushing a cart stuffed with things I'd just bought. I was acting like I forgot the row where my car was parked while I eyeballed the steel box that held the money. Encased in the exterior wall. According to Ciccio Formaggio's information, it had to be collected within a few minutes.

The armored truck punctually entered the parking lot. It was 8:30 P.M. The guards waited a couple minutes before opening the doors, making sure nothing suspicious was happening in the area. Only two of them got out, the driver and the guy who rode shotgun. The third stayed locked in the back, keeping them covered. He could shoot through the gun holes if it came to that. The two guards opened the box, took out the bags and got back into the truck in less than a minute. It would've been impossible to ease up, disarm them, keep an eye on the third guard and get away with the cash. The only solution was to eliminate them. I looked around and spotted a four-storey house with a terrace on the roof. About a hundred meters away, as the crow flies. I reached the gate and waited for somebody to show up. A woman arrived with two children. Right then I leaped out of the shadow, holding a couple shopping bags. My looks, suit, shit-eating grin, shopping all reassured her. She let me inside. I slipped up the stairs and reached the roof. Just as I expected, the terrace had a perfect view of the night safe. Two men armed with precision rifles could pick off the two guards the moment they got out of the truck. The third guard would stay trapped in the back; some shots fired at the holes would be enough to hold him off. A parked car would suddenly pull out, reach the two bodies and grab the money bags. Estimated time: one minute. I smoked another cigarette as I calculated the number of men needed for the heist. Apart from me, Ciccio and the inside guy, we'd need two crack shots on the roof and three people in the car. Eight in all. The guard and Ciccio wouldn't get a cent, so that left six cuts. Each roughly eighty-five to a hundred and twenty-five thousand. Too little to risk winding up back in jail. The players would have to be thinned out.

I got back to my car and headed towards Varese where Ciccio was waiting for me in a sandwich shop.

"So what's it look like?" he asked, a quaver in his voice.

I took a long sip of an ice-cold beer. "It'll take time to organize a hit of this size. I need to plan the operation, locate weapons, cars, hideouts, and especially the right people."

"When do you think we can do it?"

"Not before October." I aimed my finger in his face. "I'll do this job on one condition: I call the shots, and from here on out you do only what I tell you to do and nothing else."

"OK. No problem."

"You keep in touch with the inside guy. And that's it. Don't you dare take any initiatives on your own."

"Hey, pal," he shot back, offended. "This hit is my idea. Don't forget: if you get rich, you'll owe it to nobody else but me!"

I stared at him. He was a fool. "Sorry, you've got a point there. We just need to get clear from the beginning. Neither of us intends to go back to jail—right?"

"Right."

I would've loved to smoke him on the spot. I smiled and gave him a friendly pat on the back.

On the highway I started to think about how to give the slip to the Barese. If I stayed with him, I'd be his gopher forever. He couldn't care less about fucking up my life; to him I was just somebody to be used and then thrown away when I couldn't be used anymore. He was a traitor and a stoolie, and like most of us he kept to the crooked path. He had his hands in all sorts of traffic, but his blind spot was cocaine dealing. The cops in the district anti-mafia squad that kept tabs on him could overlook many things, from prostitution to loansharking, but drugs made them mad as hell, and they pulled out the handcuffs. Fact is, when it came to coke, the Barese was pretty cagey. It took me a while to find out who was supplying him. Like all hoods, he couldn't stop himself from boasting in front of the sluts he was screwing. There was a Venezuelan dancer who snorted like a vacuum cleaner: he'd promised her a stash, telling her to be patient, it'd show up in a couple days. She asked me if I could get her a taste in the meantime, tipping me off about the arrival of the shit.

On the day of the score I tailed the Barese. In the middle of the afternoon he met some olive-skinned stranger in the men's-wear section of a department store in Treviso. Using the old excuse of trying on some trousers, they both went into the same dressing room, one after the other. The courier left an elegant briefcase which my employer then picked up. The stranger went back inside to try on another pair of trousers and grabbed the cash the Barese left there. I followed the dealer to a parking lot. Took down his license number. Before going to work I indulged in a meal at a top-drawer restaurant to celebrate. The Barese now frightened me less.

I had two ways of quitting my job at the club. Sell the owner to the *Sacra Corona Unita*, who had long wanted to settle the score with the Barese for sending a boss from Taranto to jail. Or sell him to the bulls. I carefully weighed the pros and cons. I definitely couldn't make a mistake. The Pugliese mafia would've butchered him like a goat or filled him with lead, eliminating the problem at the root. But it wasn't at all clear they wouldn't also eliminate yours truly, who might one day turn into an inconvenient witness. To my thinking, the cops were less dangerous, but more complicated. The problem was which cop to trust: just like hoods, they'd use you, then throw you away. The police and the carabinieri did it because they despised you, not because they gained anything by it. With their starvation salaries, the risks and the ulcers, they saw the world divided into citizens to be protected and scum to be tossed into jail. They loathed the scum, spit in their faces, kicked them in the balls. But I did feel I could trust one cop: Anedda. Something about him always made me think he was rotten. Not just corrupt. Rotten. The right sort of guy to form a partnership with. By offering him the Barese on a silver platter I'd whet his appetite. The rest I'd propose to him later. I switched the turn signal to exit into a service area. A piss, a coffee and a phone call. Exactly in that order.

Ferruccio Anedda was truly elegant. Not only did he have good taste, but he wore his clothes naturally, without any put-on. Like a real gentleman. He'd driven three hundred kilometers and his cream-colored linen suit wasn't even creased. I cut to the chase, and he listened to me closely. When I finished, he lit the cigarette he'd been turning around between his thumb and index finger. He pocketed the slip of paper with the dealer's license number. Only then did he decide to say something: "Bravo, Giorgio Pellegrini, attaboy. You want to fuck over the Barese, and you want me to let you pinch the dough from the coke."

"That we'll split fifty-fifty," I corrected him. The words escaped my mouth in a tone that was too sharp. It was the fear I might be mistaken about what he was. "Fame and money," I added, trying to mask the tension. "Two good reasons for accepting my proposal."

Anedda was too much of an old hand to have overlooked these details. He played with my fear, looking me straight in the eye. "Seventy-thirty. Who do you think you are, asking for half?"

I spread my arms. "I beg your pardon."

We were in a country lane on the outskirts of the town.

Despite the darkness and the lowered windows, the bull's car was hot. As if the sheet metal was giving off the heat it had absorbed during the day. My shirt was glued to my back. I hated sweating. He looked as if he'd just stepped out of the shower.

"So we wait for the Barese outside the department store and nab him with the cocaine." He began to go over everything again. "In the meantime you intercept the courier in the dressing room, knock him upside the head and grab the cash. This is your plan, right?"

"Right."

"Not bad. It saves us a lot of trouble. Are you sure the exchange always happens in the same place?"

I didn't answer. I looked at the tips of my shoes. I hadn't really thought about this possibility. I felt as if I'd gone back in time to the moment when I hadn't verified the night watchman's schedule and that shithead blew himself up.

"I ask you," continued Anedda in a tone as cold as blue steel, "because I wouldn't want to move a squad from Milano, inventing a mountain of bullshit to justify the urgency and the absence of communication with colleagues in Treviso, only to have the whole thing fizzle out. Make a fool of myself. And take a lot of heat. The kind that cuts short your career. Because in that case I'll fuck you, Pellegrini. You can bet on it."

I knew I could. I had to make a quick decision. Cancel the job or guarantee there wouldn't be any surprises. I decided to take the risk. Otherwise the hit at the superstore would be no more than a missed opportunity, and as old as I was I couldn't allow myself any regrets. I could only take the risk. Besides, from a purely statistical point of view, it was unlikely I'd be handed the same tough luck twice in a row.

"Don't get worked up, Anedda," I said. "I'll get you that fame and money. For you it'll be just another job."

At the club the coke supply seemed to be never-ending. I

followed the traffic through a few customers who couldn't get enough. They owed me favors. The stress was killing me. A woman would've been just the ticket. A woman like Flora. But I'd have to wait. There are times when it's best to be on your own.

The Barese had no partners. He couldn't have. And after he fell into Anedda's hands, he'd have to say adios to Blue Skies as well as his freedom. His friends in the anti-mafia squad couldn't do fuck all for him. The Milanese bull would cover his ass with a dynamite press conference. Newspapers, radio, TV. He and his men lined up behind a table where the coke would be on eye-popping display. I told Anedda nothing interesting was happening at the club. Dancers and a couple gorillas. But as I was telling him I got an idea. Two, in fact. The first gave me the chance to settle up with the Romanians. When it rained, the arm they broke was sore as hell, reminding me of the humiliation I suffered. I told Anedda they blabbed to me about killing the Albanian at the farmhouse. The Digos officer in him pricked up his ears.

"I was just asking myself what I could give my colleagues in the area to bite the bullet and ease the pain of not getting the coke bust. Solving a homicide is always good publicity, even if the case is no big deal. Do you have any information that can nail them?"

I smiled. "They got rid of the clubs and hammers by tossing them in a ditch."

"And you just happen to know the place."

I smiled again.

The second idea concerned the assets of the club, namely the dancers. Blue Skies would be confiscated, and they'd find themselves out of work. A real shame. I could make some easy cash by selling a few to the Kosovar gangs who buzzed around the northeast in search of professional dancers for clubs in Pristina. The glorious war of liberation had ended a while ago, but the K-4 troops, the peace-keeping force, still hadn't left. And like all soldiers they wanted to be entertained and get their rocks off. So from one day to the next the Kosovar mafia, a direct offshoot of their Albanian counterparts, opened clubs of every kind. Lap dancing raked in the most cash, but it wasn't easy to find professional dancers. The major obstacle was the girls themselves, who on no account wanted to wind up in the Albanians' hands. I could close the deal by taking advantage of the confusion caused by the Barese's arrest. I couldn't unload all the girls, but five or six would be an acceptable number. I'd have to keep Anedda in the dark, I'd be taking a big risk, but the dolls would net me at least thirty thousand. I dropped by a club where the Kosovar boss hung out. He was bragging to some Italian laborers about being a hero in the Kosovo Liberation Army, an exterminator of Serbs. I pretended to listen respectfully, then offered him the deal. He accepted the figure without much haggling, said he'd send somebody to pick the girls. He was so polite I decided to show up armed when we settled.

Days passed, the stock of cocaine dwindled, and the date of my release from the Barese was getting closer. I knew the time had come to locate a hideout that was safe and secret. The cops shouldn't find me in the club. Very soon, in any case, they'd want to have a chat with me too. Until Anedda explained my situation to his colleagues, it'd be beneficial to make myself scarce. I knew only one way to locate a safe place. I started to pore over the ads in the Lombard newspapers, avoiding Bergamo and focusing on the Varese area. I wanted to find somewhere that wasn't too far from the scene of the rip-off. But as soon as I learned the Barese would meet with his supplier in ten or so days, I gave up this part of the plan and fell back on an old acquaintance: the gangster's widow. She owned a place in Milano, a detail she spilled to me when she still didn't get the kind of guy I was. I went knocking on the door of the room she'd taken in a Udine hotel. She was entertaining a sixty-something. When he spotted me, he knew he'd better get dressed and disappear. But she didn't put on a stitch. She looked for a cigarette on the nightstand and sat on the edge of the unmade bed. "What do you want?" she asked, running a hand through her hair.

I didn't answer. Had a look around. A pig sty. "With all the money I gave you, you could afford something better."

She shook her head. Through the movement of her hair, I saw a bitter grimace ravage her face. It lasted no more than an instant, long enough to realize she was in my grip again. My dough had so disgusted her she gambled it all away. Down to the last euro.

"So you blew it at the casino?"

"I wish. A backroom game was enough."

I didn't have much time. I increased the dose. "And now you're broke again, forced to service retirees."

"What do you want?" she repeated.

"I want you to get on a train, go back to your place in Milano and put me up for a couple months. I'll pay you well."

She stared at me. She knew I was looking for a hideout. Definitely a hood's widow. "But no funny business. I'm fed up with your garbage," she hissed like a snake.

Maybe the lady felt entitled to think we could switch roles, seeing as how I needed her apartment. Her skittish rebellion turned me on as I hadn't been for ages. I took in the wrinkles on her neck, her sagging tits, the puckers of cellulite around her thighs. I pulled her by the hair and made her stretch out on the bed, face down. From the nightstand I grabbed the bottle of Fernet Branca she used to rinse out her mouth after blowjobs, and I wedged it delicately between her buttocks. My hand remained motionless for an endless minute. I wanted her to be completely aware of what she was about to suffer. She took it like a pro. She knew she was a loser, stuck on the bottom rung of the ladder that was her scene. She was trying her best to show me she'd fallen in line again.

I tipped Anedda the exchange would go down within forty-eight hours. He told me he identified the courier from the license number. The car belonged to an Italian woman, a resident of Milano who was formerly a streetwalker, now retired. She lived with somebody called Jesus Zamorano, a Bolivian with a record for drug dealing.

That same night the bull arrived with his squad, a group of forty-year-olds with the look of experts. They belonged to the anti-terrorist generation: they were the ones who chased us down and kicked our asses. We met in the parking lot of a pensione, on Venetian terra firma. Anedda made me a sign to follow him. He handed me some contraption that looked like a cross between a cell phone and a straight razor.

"It's a stun gun," he explained. "Stick it in the Bolivian's ribs, press the button, and he'll hit the ground, out of commission for about ten minutes."

"I would've preferred a real gun."

He snorted with impatience. "It's better to avoid a shoot-out and corpses in a department store. This thing is more discreet."

Suddenly I got it. "You don't have any intention of nabbing the courier."

"Of course not. He's my gift to some Milanese colleagues. I owe them a couple favors. You need to be generous in these cases. Busting the Barese will make a big enough splash."

Things were hopping at the club that night, and the Barese was smiling, satisfied with the way business was going. I would've liked to know where he stashed the loot. Maybe abroad. But he didn't strike me as a guy who wanted to be far from his cash. Blue Skies was a real gold mine, and I guessed he put aside at least a million. He'd drop a wad on the lawyers, but he'd have more than enough left to get by. Once he got out of jail.

Some bruiser tapped me on the shoulder. It was the Kosovar who came to pick the girls. He sized them up for a while, then pointed out seven.

"That's thirty-five grand." My tone was gruff.

"No problem, bud."

I avoided eye contact so he wouldn't see I knew they wanted to fuck me over. They planned to take away the dancers without shelling out a cent. I sure as hell couldn't show up at the meeting armed with the stun gun Anedda gave me. They'd slit my throat. I decided if I couldn't find a more suitable weapon, I'd call off the deal.

The last customers left the club at four. I dashed home. Packed my bags and stowed them in the Panda. After a few hours' sleep, I jumped into the shower and drove to Treviso. I checked the battery on my cell phone for the zillionth time. Anedda was going to ring me as soon as the Barese got close to the store.

The call came a little after eleven. I was wandering around the housewares section on the top floor.

"He's on his way in," the cop warned me.

I slowly approached the escalator. From above I spotted the Bolivian strolling between the shelves of toys. He also got a phone call and headed for men's wear.

They used the same dressing room to make the exchange. As the Barese walked away with the cocaine, I reached the closed door. Behind it the courier was probably counting the cash. When he opened it, I poked the stun gun in his chest, and he collapsed without a whimper. I stepped inside, closing the door behind me. Checked the brief case. Full of banknotes. I frisked Zamorano: under his jacket, on his left side, he was carrying a sawed-off shotgun. A forty-centimeter toy loaded with shot for boar-hunting. The ideal weapon to bring to a business meeting with the Kosovar mafia. I left the dressing room and quickly walked away, taking the stairs. On the street I noticed a good deal of confusion. A crowd of on lookers surrounded two unmarked police cars. I got to the parking lot, hid the briefcase and shotgun under the seat and drove back to town, careful to avoid the slightest infraction of the traffic code. I got to Blue Skies, which was empty at that hour, and commandeered the van they used to make all kinds of deliveries. The previous night I snatched the keys that were always next to the cash register. I started rounding up the dancers who'd been picked to work in the clubs in Pristina. They all lived around there. I knocked on door after door, telling them a dragnet was in process and the Barese had ordered me to hide them. None of the girls found it strange. The tale was believable, after all. The van had no windows in the back, and they couldn't see where I was taking them. I was meeting the Kosovars in the parking lot of a shopping center outside Mestre. A gang of five guys led by the bruiser who showed at the club. They started to walk towards me, smiling. Immediately I saw what was coming. They'd surround me, giving me a warm welcome, and one of them would stab me. Discreetly. A lunge at the heart, the blade skillfully slipped between the ribs. Then they'd hold me up, like a friend too drunk to stay on his feet, and push me into a car. I beat them to it: I leaned my back up against the van and pulled the shotgun out from under my jacket. The thugs stopped short, keeping their hands in plain view. True professionals. The message was clear: a request for a truce so we could deal. Sweat was streaming down my face and neck. It ran into my eyes and burned the hell out of them, but I wasn't going to lower the gun for anything.

A lady and a gent passed by, pushing a shopping cart. They got the drift and took off.

"Money tomorrow," said the leader. "Today not possible."

"You ugly mother fuckers. You wanted to rip me off. Beat it or I'll shoot."

They piled into two high-powered cars and burned rubber as they left. I threw open the sliding door of the van.

"Out," I shouted at the girls. "The club's been shut down. Go find another job."

The shotgun I still held in my hand was the most persuasive argument for them. They hightailed it, no questions asked. I climbed into the van, wracked by anger and fear. I hit my forehead with the palm of my hand. Hard. To hurt myself. What a dope I'd been. For a shitty thirty-five thousand I risked getting killed. In future I'd have to be less reckless. Otherwise I'd never make it.

FRANCISCA

I HAD TO LEAVE THE WIDOW'S PLACE to meet Anedda. But I couldn't leave her alone with my money. In that fucking apartment I couldn't even find a decent hole to hide it. Once the old floozy was alone, she'd jump at the chance to rummage through my bags and blow my savings at the nearest casino. I searched for some solution. In the end I went to buy a baby bottle in the pharmacy downstairs and a liter of Fernet in a grocery. The widow was taking a bath. I held her nose shut, stuffed two sleeping pills into her mouth and chased them with the nipple.

"Suck," I ordered.

She probably thought this was one of my pranks. She obeyed, frightened. She couldn't wait for me to take off and leave her in peace. I sat on the edge of the tub and lit two cigarettes. Slipped one between her lips.

"Don't dream of spitting up."

In her eyes I saw she wanted to let loose one of her typically unpleasant remarks. But she held back. More from resignation, I think, than fear. I waited about ten minutes. So she wouldn't drown, I removed the stopper and the water started to drain.

"When I come back, I want to find you here."

"Let me go to bed. I'll have a long sleep. Soaking wet I might catch cold."

I sighed. I was in no mood to make concessions. "No. Stay put."

Ferruccio the bull told me to meet him outside the McDonald's in front of the central train station. I had a vise-grip on the briefcase with the money. All of it. It was up to him to give me my thirty percent. A gang leader's role instead of a cop's. You start off like a shining knight, but in time you get your hands dirty, not to mention your heart and brain. He pulled up in a Fiat Brava. Stuck his hand out the window to signal me to get in.

"Have you seen the papers?" he asked, pleased with himself.

I shook my head.

"And the TV?" he insisted.

"I don't watch it, and I don't read newspapers. I couldn't give a fuck."

"What a shame. The operation got loads of attention, and my colleagues in Veneto had to chill out. The chief of police personally complimented me."

I nodded ceremoniously. Anedda parked on a side street with little traffic. He pointed at the briefcase. "How much?"

"Two hundred on the nose."

He elbowed me in the cheekbone. A sharp jab, precise and powerful, delivered with an ease that comes from practice and training. My vision went blurry, and I leaned my forehead on the dashboard.

"I heard about some strange goings-on in a parking lot in Mestre," he hissed in a rage. "Some dude with a sawed-off shotgun held off a gang of assholes, while a bunch of trashy broads busted out the back of a van and took off in every direction like a flock of chickens."

It was no use contradicting him. Anedda would've taken me out. "I did something stupid."

He elbowed me again, this time in the ear. An interrogation technique. In his long and honored career, he must've beaten quite a few leftwing students and workers. I knew he needed to vent and it was better to keep quiet.

"You wanted to rip me off, but because you're such a prick-head, you risked fucking everything up. If the carabinieri or the revenue officers had collared you, we would've all wound up in jail."

He pulled the key from the ignition and raked it across my cheek. In silence I took out my handkerchief and tamped the wound. I lowered the visor, wiped the dust off the mirror with my fingers, and checked the cut. A couple centimeters long. No big deal. Just something to clarify our relationship now and in future.

"You need to be taught a lesson," the cop went on more calmly. "Instead of thirty your share'll be ten percent."

I shook my head. "Give me thirty, and I'll let you in on something that'll make you rich."

"What is it?" he gibed. "Another close-out sale on whores?"

"An armored truck."

He lit a cigarette. "How much?"

"Half a million for sure, maybe three quarters."

"I'm listening."

"I want thirty percent."

"You'll get it only if the offer interests me."

I told him everything, without leaving out a single detail.

"What do you want from me?" he asked when I finished. "You don't expect me to put on a ski mask, do you?"

"Of course not," I came right back. "You'd only have to show me which people to contact for the heist. I'm out of circulation. And I don't want to turn to the hoods I met at San Vittore. They know who I am, but I don't trust them. If something goes wrong, they'll squeal right away."

"And that's it?"

"There's one more thing, but it has nothing to do with pulling off the heist. Let's just say it'll make divvying up the take easier."

He sneered. "How many you want to knock out?"

"Two are already dead, but they don't know it yet. The jury's still out on the others. I was thinking of getting them all together for the split . . . and then using your help to dole out some lead."

He pulled out a gun and poked it in my side. "You might get the idea to kill me too."

"The idea might be mutual."

Ferruccio slipped the Beretta back into his holster and changed the subject. "So you want me to get you some desperate characters, guys with nothing to lose."

"Hard to find?"

He burst out laughing. "Not at all. Once they were rare, but now they go by the kilo. This country has turned into an elephant cemetery: they all come here to die."

He grew serious again and started counting the cash. He stuffed my share into a paper bag and told me to beat it. He'd get in touch on the cell phone. He didn't ask where I was staying. Either he already knew or he didn't give a fuck.

I hailed a taxi and had him drop me two hundred meters from the widow's place. I found her still in dreamland. I lifted her bodily out of the tub and laid her on the bed. Then I went back to the bathroom to look at myself in the mirror. The cheek was swollen, but the wound had stopped bleeding. I ransacked the cabinet and found disinfectant and bandages. I'd have a scar. In an emergency room a surgeon could've closed the flaps of skin with a few stitches, but the cut looked exactly like what it was: mutilation. Better avoid any complications. The house was quiet. I threw myself into an armchair and smoked a cigarette. I had to solve the problem of stashing my savings. I couldn't put the widow to sleep every time I went out. What with the pills and the Fernet I'd kill her. Too soon. I always thought she'd have to die. After the robbery I couldn't leave behind a blabbermouth. At this point she knew diddly squat, but she'd hung around hoods too long not to link my stay in Milano with the hit on the armored truck. A heist worth half a million euros with two dead bodies on the tarmac isn't the sort of news that passes unnoticed. If Ciccio Formaggio had to be eliminated because he might let slip one word too many, the widow was sure as shit to talk. For revenge. For the satisfaction of holding her head up one last time. I'd have to find a way of getting rid of her without rousing suspicion. The neighbors had already noticed me. I stood up and began to wander around the joint, searching for a hiding place. In one room I found a wardrobe that was too heavy for her to move by herself. I went back to the bedroom to make sure she was still asleep. I divided the cash into bundles and slipped them into freezer bags. Then I tacked them to the back of the wardrobe. I pushed it against the wall and checked to make sure the bags couldn't be spotted. It wasn't such a hot moneybox, but I didn't have anything better at hand.

I changed my clothes. The widow had woken up but pretended to be asleep so she wouldn't have to deal with me.

"I'm going out. You stay put and watch TV. You're paid to do this too."

When I reached the street, it hit me I didn't know where to go. I had no desire to revisit the spots where I used to hang as an ex-con, flat broke and desperate. I started walking aimlessly. It was a pleasant evening at the end of September, and I walked on and on, window-shopping, people-watching. I stopped in a restaurant filled with people eating, drinking, chattering away. I was the only one who had nothing to do but take in the scene. I was on pins and needles till the waiter served me my risotto. At a certain point, the chef came out of the kitchen. From the way he acted I guessed he was also the owner. He began to go from table to table, asking customers if the dishes met with their approval. Occasionally he'd sit for a few minutes and make small talk. It was a gracious gesture that people appreciated. My turn came. The guy sized me up, figured I was just a chance customer, and went no further than to ask me quietly whether I was pleased with the meal and the service.

Without answering I pointed to the chair on my right. "May I offer you a glass of wine?"

He was taken aback for a moment; then he satisfied me. With a wave he had a glass brought to him.

"I used to work in a place that served food and drink," I told him. "Like you, I was treated with respect by the customers. You know what I mean?"

The chef nodded and adjusted his neckerchief. He was about fifty, thin but muscular. His smock was spotless, and his hands were clean and well cared for. A winner.

"Seeing as how I'd like to get into a different line of work," I went on, "I asked myself if opening a restaurant might be a good investment. Of course I like working with people—"

He emptied his glass. He didn't have the slightest intention of talking to me. "I don't know where you worked before, what sort of place it might have been, but being a restaurateur is a serious matter," he began to explain in a smart-aleck tone. "One must know the trade and have a broad knowledge of the wine industry as well. Perhaps a pizzeria would be a more suitable venture. Good or bad, everybody eats pizza," he concluded as he stood up. He politely held out his hand and went over to another table.

"Pizzeria my asshole," I thought as I kept my eyes on him. I wasn't going to invest my money in some third-rate business. These days even the Chinese were opening pizzerias. With the risks I was running to guarantee myself a decent future, I deserved something better. I needed a good reputation, and only the finest people could provide me with that. The ones with the fat wallets and the right circle of friends. I'd open a classy place. Obviously without trying to act the part of a restaurateur. I'd limit myself to hiring professionals, and I'd be the boss, dividing my time between the account books and the customers' tables. It was only a question of money. When you're on the fringes with time in the slammer, life's an uphill race. And everything costs double.

I paid the check and hit the street again. When I got tired, I ducked into a movie theater. An American picture. Boring.

I went back to the widow's. When she heard the key turn in the lock, she ran to shut herself up in her room. For a moment I was tempted to leave her in peace, but I was bored stiff and wanted to amuse myself. I knocked on the door. I made her come back to the living room—on all fours.

Ferruccio the bull didn't contact me for a week. On Saturday I cased the superstore again to verify the schedule and movements of the armored truck. But it was the only time I managed to shake off the boredom. The city spat me out like a foreign body, and my only distraction was restaurants. Two a day. I only went into the ones that seemed top-notch to me.

Same McDonald's as last time and same car. Anedda drove fast in traffic, constantly checking the rear-view mirror. He was always on the look-out.

"I found the right people," he announced. "Three Spanish anarchists, two men and a woman. On the run from another robbery. And no way to beat the rap."

"Who else?" I pressed him.

He chuckled. "Two Ustashi Croats. War criminals. But perfect shots."

I shook my head. "It won't work. They'll never agree to work together."

"Oh yes they will," Ferruccio shot back. "They're real desperate, and they need the cash. Besides, they don't have to work together. The Croats will be on the roof and the Spaniards in the car retrieving the money bags."

It rang true. Not a bad idea. "And even if they croak, nobody's going to give a damn, right?"

"Right. Under the seat are two files with all the information about them, including photos and current addresses. There was enough to arrest them, but I managed to change the program. You've got ten minutes to read the files. I can't let them go."

I started with the Croats. Romo Dujc, alias Cerni the Black Shirt, 44, and Tonci Zaninovic, 42. Soldiers in the seventy-second battalion of the military police. Charged with participating in various ethnic cleansing operations. The report indicated they were snipers. This was the only detail that interested me. I studied their photos. Ugly. Dangerous. It wouldn't be easy to get rid of them. They were holed up in the Giambellino quarter, in a small apartment rented to a Croat prostitute. Patriotic solidarity.

I shifted to the Spaniards. Sebastián Monrubia, 39, Esteban Collar, 36, and María Garcés, 31. Noms de guerre: Pepe, Javier and Francisca. She was a fly piece of ass; the other two wore the grim looks of militants sworn to self-sacrifice. Whacking them wouldn't be a problem. The Spanish authorities were after them for a robbery that went south, one cop dead, another seriously wounded. They were hiding out at the home of an Italian comrade who hung around a community center. His phone was tapped.

I put the files back under the seat and lit a cigarette. "I'll contact both groups tomorrow."

"How do you plan to approach them?"

I expected that question. It was the most difficult step in the operation. The pretext had to be convincing. Very convincing. "I'll tell them I'm an informer, and I've picked them out. But since they're such a slick crew, I won't sell them to the cops. Instead I'll let them in on a robbery that's a sure thing and very profitable."

Anedda turned to look at me. "Can't you think of something less dangerous? They don't strike me as people who take kindly to informers. You're risking a bullet in the belly."

I shrugged my shoulders. "It'll be hard to make them swallow the idea that some crook has tracked them down. Better a half-truth."

The cop let me out at the Cadorna station. I walked till I got hungry. Then I went into a restaurant.

I rang the bell of the Croats' hide-out at eight in the morning. I chose to confront them when they were still groggy from sleep. The girl answered. Her surname was Bazov, her Christian name unpronounceable. On the street she called herself Luana. There's nothing worse than a whore with a complicated name. She came from Vukovar. A refugee in her country, a refugee in Italy, then the life. She opened the door with her eyes half-closed. "What do you want?" she mumbled.

"From you, nothing. I want to talk to Cerni and his partner, Zaninovic."

She turned a whiter shade of pale, then sprang back wide-awake. She shook her head, on the edge of panic. "I don't know these men," she lied.

I gave her a nasty pinch on a nipple. Another little trick I learned from the two Romanians at the club. "Go call them," I ordered.

Scared, she slammed the door in my face. I could've given it a push and forced my way into the apartment, but I couldn't rule out the possibility the two guys were there eavesdropping, armed and ready for anything. I sensed the presence of somebody eyeing me through the peephole. I didn't move a muscle. It was Cerni himself who opened the door. One hand on the knob, the other holding a large automatic.

"Ciao, Romo," I greeted him. "I want to talk to you."

He stuck out his head to make sure I was alone. Then he fastened his eyes on me. He was strapping, his face creepy. His girlish mouth fought against his shaved skull, his skinhead sideburns and the sagging flesh on his chin. Pale blue eyes. Shifty, like a hunted animal's. When I looked into them, I knew for certain this fucker wouldn't go down easy before he gave us his slice of the pie.

He nodded at me to get inside. As soon as I stepped over the threshold, he slammed me against the wall and frisked me. He did it like a pro. After all, he'd been in the military police for a good part of his life. He directed me into the hallway with the gun. We went into a roomy kitchen where his partner was waiting for us, armed with a pump rifle. He aimed it at my face. If he squeezed the trigger, my head would've been ripped from my body. Romo barked an order, and Tonci lowered the weapon. I smiled at him. He was tall and thin, with muscles sculpted by years at the gym. His head was shaved too. He had a pig's face and a pointy blond goatee. The classic executioner. They steered me towards a chair. The table was still set from the night before. Plates and cutlery for two. The girl must be on the street before dinner. I lit a cigarette.

"Talk," ordered Cerni in Italian. He sounded like a cop. The job must've been imprinted in his DNA.

"I work for the police," I explained. "I help the bulls hunt down fugitives. For money. I'm not a patriot like you. I tracked you down, but instead of selling you out I thought I'd offer you a job."

Cerni translated for his buddy. Then he set his eyes on me again. "What kind of job?"

"A robbery. An armored truck."

"We've never done a robbery."

"You only have to stand on a roof and pick off two guards." I made the gesture of aiming and firing. "Snipers," I added.

They muttered to one another. "How much money for each of us?"

"Not less than a hundred thousand. With that kind of cash you could guarantee yourselves a decent escape."

"Why should we trust you?"

"Because you're in deep shit. If you're forced to hide abroad, it means your friends at home have unloaded you. You've been judged expendable, and the only way to save your asses is to find enough dough to cross the ocean and leave Europe behind."

"What if we don't accept the offer, maybe because we don't trust you? Informers betray everybody, with no exceptions."

"Then you better find another hideout because the cops'll be here soon."

Romo sneered. "We could kill you now so you won't go tell your friends, the cops."

I shook my head and put on a rueful look. "You disappoint me. I took you for smarter. You really think I'd come here without taking the necessary precautions?"

He stood up. Grabbed a bottle of beer from the fridge. "I don't like having to trust an informer."

"You've got no choice." I cut him short, my tone hard. "I didn't sell you out because you're crack shooters, and the robbery earns me more. That's it."

They talked to one another again. Of the two, Tonci seemed more pliable.

Romo scratched his bristly beard. "OK, we're in. But watch your step, Dago: we'll get even."

I dismissed the threat with a wave and proceeded to lay out the details of the heist. I learned they commanded a pretty good arsenal. It contained two Russian precision rifles, Dragunovs, with ten-shot clips and infrared sights. You take a liking to the tools of your trade and never get rid of them.

Romo translated Tonci's question about how the loot would be divided. They weren't stupid. Already spotted the moment when they'd be most vulnerable. My answer: I still had to work it out. Romo made clear they wouldn't do the job without knowing all the details. I told them not to worry and headed for the door.

I had a coffee to unwind. Those two guys gave me the willies. Dangerous fanatics, pros at inflicting violence and cruelty. Going back over the conversation, word by word, I reached the conclusion they'd try to snatch the whole purse. They had nothing to lose and might decide not to leave any witnesses hanging around. The meeting to split the cash risked turning into a shoot-out. My plan, however, anticipated an execution.

I decided to look up the Spaniards. Took the tram. Always preferred to travel by public transport. That way I could more easily make out whether I was being followed. Besides, I liked looking at the city through the window, checking out streets and the traffic.

Nobody was home. Their host had to be at work. Since it was eleven in the morning, I thought they might be in the neighborhood doing some shopping—if they hadn't decided to stay in shape by knocking off a bank. Found them in a bar instead. As I passed by the window I spotted them, busy biting into cornetti and drinking cappuccini and frappés. I went inside, grabbed a chair and sat at their table. The two men reacted by slipping their hands into their jacket pockets, searching for the reassuring butts of their guns. I challenged them with a look. The woman did nothing but stare at me. She was the leader. No doubt about it. I rested my hands on the table to show I didn't have any bad intentions.

"Pepe, Javier and Francisca. Pleased to make your acquaintance," I said in a friendly tone, speaking Spanish and using their noms de guerre.

"Who are you?" she asked.

"Somebody who knows everything about you."

"You're a comrade?" asked Pepe.

I sneered. "Once upon a time I was. Now I've stopped dreaming and dedicated myself to making money."

"Who are you?" repeated Francisca. "You speak Spanish like a Mexican."

I gave her the once-over. She was a stinger, really beautiful. Dark hair and eyes. Perfectly oval face. Big tits. Long legs sticking out of a miniskirt. The low-heeled shoes didn't go with the outfit: she probably wore them in case they had to make tracks. What a shame she wasn't my type. Not only was she too young, but she came off like one of those ballbreakers who never knuckle under. Especially to a man.

I ignored her questions and ordered my third coffee of the morning from the barista. Lit a cigarette. Only then did I speak. "I'm a police informer. I would've sold you to the cops, but it's just your luck I need you for a certain job."

"What kind of job?" asked the woman.

"A robbery. An armored truck. One hundred thousand a head."

The three of them looked at each other. The two men were pointing their guns at me through their jacket pockets. They would've been happy to fire, but the place was too crowded.

"We don't work with scum," said Francisca.

I smiled and looked her in the eye. "Then start running," I flashed back, pointing at the door. "You can bet your little Italian friend, his girl and the people at the community center are going to have a rough time."

"Motherfucker." Pepe insulted me. "They know nothing about us. They think we're three Spanish comrades on vacation."

"I know the score. You think the police and the judges won't jump on 'a new criminal element in the area' to square accounts with a community center that's always breaking balls?

Won't be the first time it's happened in Italy. It's business as usual."

I watched them. I knew perfectly well what they were thinking. Others would've hit the door and felt no qualms if somebody wound up in jail. But not comrades. Consistency, a sense of responsibility, militant solidarity. I recognized their confusion. It was identical to what I'd read in Gianni's face at that Parisian brasserie. They'd accept my offer. They couldn't carry the shame of a betrayal to the grave. Good for them. They'd die happy.

"Fuck off," ordered the woman. "We have to talk. We'll meet here tomorrow, same time."

I walked till lunch. I chose a restaurant carefully and phoned Ferruccio the bull. He asked me where I was. Twenty minutes later I saw him come in, impeccable and elegant as always. The wine I'd chosen wasn't to his liking. He had it switched without asking my opinion. A cop's cockiness.

"Did they go for it?" he asked.

I told the whole story, down to the smallest details. As I always did with him. Even shared my suspicions about the Croats' plan to whack us and make off with the cash.

"The Spaniards might also be tempted," Anedda figured. "This way they could lay out two Croatian fascists and a police informer."

I hadn't thought of this. His reasoning was flawless, but I knew too much about far-left idealists to think it had a real chance of happening. Still, to be on the safe side, it was best not to take anything for granted.

"When we split the cash, you'll have to be there, hidden, ready to show at the right moment to help me smoke them."

"Seven's too many," he remarked.

"Five," I corrected. "Ciccio Formaggio and his inside guy will check out the night before."

"You'll see to it?"

"Yes."

He adjusted the knot in his tie. "Five's not so few, but it can be done. We'll have to find an abandoned house in the country."

"That's your job. You're the Milanese."

For the umpteenth time he discreetly surveyed the joint, searching for faces he recognized. Reassured, he stood up and left without paying his share of the bill.

The widow had gotten drunk. I found her stretched out on the couch, face down. The room stank of smoke and liquor. I threw open a window. Made some strong coffee and filled the tub with cold water. That bitch drank just to dodge me.

The next morning only María Garcés, alias Francisca, showed up at the bar. Her hair was tied back, and she wore jeans that accentuated her ass and legs.

"Alone?"

"Better one in jail than three."

"Right. You can never be too careful. So what did you decide?"

"We can't let someone innocent pay for us. The problem is you offer no guarantee of safety. This could be a trap. After the heist you shoot us in the back or turn us over to the police. And once we're gone you can denounce our Italian comrades. With scum like you we can never be sure."

She enjoyed insulting me. She was indignant, angry, especially because she knew I had them boxed in. "If you're finished with the bullshit, we can move on and discuss the plan." I spelled out the operation without saying the place and date, just as I'd done with the Croats. When she asked me who the other players were, I mentioned only Romo and Tonci. As soon as she heard they were Ustashi, she started to spew insults. I let her vent for a while. She chilled out when I told her after the split they could slit each other's throats if they liked. From her expression I could tell the Spaniards had also considered this angle. Ferruccio saw right through them. Apart from that idiot Ciccio Formaggio and the inside guy, all the other players were keen to eliminate the competition. But I wasn't worried at all about the Spaniards. No, the Croats were the ones who bothered me. And Anedda. He was an unknown quantity. I thought him capable of anything. Even of saving the last bullet in the clip for me, once the others were eliminated. I had no intention of laying him out. In days to come he could still be useful. But I'd have to keep my eye on him, and if he wanted to try and fuck me over, I'd pay him back in the same coin.

"I want to see the place and the armored truck when it collects the money. I want to check the escape routes." The Spaniard started making a list, distracting me from my thoughts.

I shut her up with a wave. "I'll show you a video. I don't want any fugitives buzzing around my hit. You might fuck everything up. It goes down in ten days." On Saturday I'd film the whole scenario with a video camera, and the following week we'd enter the field.

She stared at me, boiling with hatred. "More and more this robbery stinks like a trap."

"The only thing it stinks like is money, but you're too obsessed with your role as the true blue militant to realize it."

She raised a hand to slap me. "We're in a bar," I calmly reminded her.

She lowered it. "Try and fuck us, and it'll be the last mistake you make."

I sighed. She was unbearable. It'd be a pleasure to blow her away. I cracked a smile. "We'll meet here in exactly one week, same time. And bring your little friends. I'll introduce you to the rest of the group."

I met Ciccio Formaggio for lunch. He started to grumble

when he caught the prices on the menu. "Where the fuck have you brought me? I can't remember the last time I got fleeced like this."

I snorted. "What balls! You're about to fill your pockets with thousands, and you whine about a restaurant bill?"

He turned chipper again. "So how's it going?"

"Aces. Just a few practical details to take care of."

"What should I do?"

"Steal two cars. Make them four-doors. No wrecks. Then park them in two garages far away from each other, and give me the receipts."

"That's it?"

"Well, no," I answered with a wink. "You have to come with the inside guy to get your share of the cash—and enjoy it."

"Where do we meet?"

"I'll tell you when you give me the receipts."

I learned how to work the video camera in a hurry. Paid a lot of dough for it. Had to have sharp images to show the rest of the gang. When the armored truck pulled up to collect the week's take, I was on the roof of the building where I'd position the Croats. Ready to shoot a short subject that was going to gross three quarters of a million. I got inside with a master key Ciccio Formaggio had somebody cut for me the night before. It was already dark, but the lights in the parking lot shone bright as day. Like the other times, the truck stopped a couple minutes with the motor running. The doors opened, and the two guards got out with their hands on the butts of their guns. Large semi-automatics, with a combined firepower of thirty shots. Weapons suited for a shoot-out with a visible enemy at close range, but not to defend yourself against shells fired by marks-men. They were wearing bulletproof vests, but even those couldn't do much against Romo and Tonci's highcaliber rifles. The jacketed shells would cut straight through the vest like a knife through butter. The snipers, in any case, would aim at the head. The two guards would collapse on the ground, slaughtered like steers at the butcher's. Attacking armored trucks in Italy was highly remunerative and far from complicated. You just needed to locate the weak point in the route and kill most of the guards. You also had to have the balls to risk prison. The two guards opened the steel box and picked up the money bags. Through the viewfinder I followed the truck till it disappeared around a curve. Just to play safe I looked at the film again. Perfect.

I'd arranged the meeting at a gambling house in the Navigli area. On Sunday morning it was deserted, and the owner, some lowlife I met in San Vittore, rented it to me for a hundred euros. When I unlocked the door, I was hit by a blast of air that stank of smoke, sweat and bad luck. I threw open all the windows in a useless attempt to air out the room. The furniture was basic: round plastic tables covered with green cloths and old rickety wooden chairs. The only new things were the television and the VCR. Beside it, on the floor, was a stack of porno cassettes. Something for the gamblers to pass the time with while they waited to play. I lit a cigarette and stood at the window to scope out the street. The Croats showed up first. Cagey, hands thrust in their pockets, ready to draw their guns and shoot. I waited for them at the door. With my hands in plain view I invited them to nose around the apartment. Far from being reassured, they planted themselves on a couch from where they could keep an eye on the entrance. The Spaniards arrived half an hour late. Pepe and Javier came in holding revolvers behind their backs and positioned themselves on each side of the door. Only then did Francisca make her appearance. That day she was even more beautiful. She wore an elegant suit, matching shoes and bag, and sheer black stockings. She didn't deem me worthy of a glance. She stopped in the middle of the room and stared at the two Croats. Romo and Tonci stared back at her. Cerni's dark expression troubled me. He liked the Spaniard. He would've enjoyed raping and then murdering her. In Central America I had the chance to gain firsthand knowledge of mercenaries, and I knew I wasn't wrong. In the end, I didn't give a damn about what happened to her, but I didn't want the heist to turn sour because of a fuck. When the Croats realized the beautiful woman's escorts were holding guns, they drew their own weapons and laid them on their knees. You could cut through the tension.

"Stash the heat," I told them firmly, "and concentrate on the plan. Next Saturday we make the hit." I darkened the room and played the VCR. The images began to move across the screen, focusing everybody's attention and easing the stress. I showed the video without interruption, then rolled it again, using stills to discuss details. The whole thing moved at a snail's pace because Tonci needed his partner's translations. But when it was over, they were all convinced the plan would work.

On a map I indicated the street that led to the superstore and the escape route. The Croats and the Spaniards had to use the two cars stolen by Ciccio Formaggio, and after the hit they were to meet me at a service station on the road to Varese. I'd guide them to a house in the country where we'd split the loot. Then everybody was on his own.

The anarchists got up and left the room. Francisca turned back to stare straight into Romo's eyes. She knew what the Ustashi was thinking, and her response lay in that look of defiance. The man, not impressed in the least, flitted his tongue.

The Croats waited ten minutes before leaving without a word. I smoked a cigarette. Removed the cassette from the VCR and crushed it with my foot. No use saving incriminating evidence. I put the pieces in a plastic bag, where I also emptied the butt-filled ashtrays. I made sure the room showed no trace of our presence. Then I left. Walked the deserted streets to the bar where the owner of the gambling house waited for me. Into his hand I slipped the key and the other half of the money I owed him.

I headed towards the centro. I needed to think over things calmly. I picked a restaurant that specialized in fish. I was hungry and ordered an antipasto misto, hot and cold, linguine with lobster, fried seppie and calamari. The sommelier arrived. With remarkable hauteur he recommended a white wine from the Collio region. While he was extolling its qualities, I glanced at the menu and saw it cost thirty euros. For that price it had to be good. With a nod I declared my agreement with his choice.

When I was finally alone, I stared at the deformed image of my face in the silver charger. Then I mentally compiled a list of the people who had to die. The widow, Ciccio Formaggio, the inside guy, Romo, Tonci, Pepe, Javier and Francisca. Eight. Too many if they were linked. But this wouldn't happen. And the foreigners' bodies would never be found. Fugitives even as corpses. I'd have to deal with the first three personally. Halfway into the antipasto I solved the problem of the widow. She'd be put to sleep with the usual method. Fernet and pills. Then, pulling her by the legs, I'd slip her body into the water till it covered her head. The neighbors, used to her long absences, won't suspect anything, and when the stench persuades them to call the police, everybody—the medical examiner included—will think it an accident. The press will recall whose wife she'd been and devote a short notice to her, seasoned with memories and compassion. I'd kill her Tuesday morning, three days after the heist, once the dust settled. Then I'd move to Veneto and start a new life. Thinking about the widow made my cock hard, and a few ways of amusing myself crossed my mind. But better let it go. If an alert corpse butcher found any trace of my little games during the autopsy, he might get some strange ideas.

The other two would die the night before the heist, Friday. I'd ask Ciccio to come and give me the keys, along with the inside guy. If he asked why we had to meet, I'd tell him I wanted to have a face-to-face with his partner before we split the cash, just to avoid any ugly surprises. It was a shitty excuse. Only a dope like Ciccio Formaggio would go for it. The guard would fall in line because he had a clean record and no criminal experience. Besides, Ciccio would reassure him. As I sucked a lobster claw, I thought about how to do them. Always pick the easiest, quickest and cleanest method. In this case, a shot in the head was the best solution. The bullet rips apart the brain, and the victim doesn't even have time to kiss tomorrow goodbye. The muck— blood, bone fragments, brain matter— sprays from the side opposite the entry wound. I'd sit in the back seat of their car and smoke them. First the driver. Then the guy beside him. With a silencer. When I executed Luca in Central America, the blast was deafening. Almost ruined the sense of wonder and power you feel when you pull a trigger and take somebody's life. Finally I'd douse the bodies with gas, so the cops'd take time identifying the charred remains. Once they learned the bodies belonged to some turncoat ex-terrorist and a security guard, they'd immediately link the double homicide to the robbery. That's just what I wanted. The trail wouldn't go anywhere, and anyhow Anedda, as a Digos officer, would take part in the investigation, keeping them off the scent if need be.

The other five, the Croats and the Spaniards, were a different story. Killing them was risky. Calculated, but still a risk. You had to shoot people who expected to be shot and were perfectly capable of shooting back. But I'd get out. Alive. Not them. They'd never get another chance to taste fried seppie and calamari like the waiter just brought me. Steaming hot and so tender they melt in your mouth. I'd lead them to the house. Anedda would jump out of his nest and spray them with lead. In the meantime I'd draw the shotgun and do my part. The best moment, of course, would be later, when we split the loot. But there was the risk they'd see it coming. And a chance the money might get ruined, stained with blood or hit by gunfire. We'd bury the bodies. Their names and faces would remain on the books as fugitives for another twenty years.

I finished with a slice of Neapolitan pastiera. The sommelier showed up again to recommend a Sicilian dessert wine to accompany it. To avoid a mini-lecture on sweet wines, I told him right away that was one of my favorites. Now was the time to go through the schedule. Every military operation must work like a Swiss watch. And knocking back an armored truck with a chaser of ten killings—this was a real operation. I went over every step again, and when I paid the bill, I felt different. Rich. A winner. That's just how I felt.

LUANA

*M*ONDAY *14:00*

Anedda was nervous. In a hurry. They were waiting for him at police headquarters to set up a bust. Algerian terrorists holed up in a safe house. A bunch of fanatics who liked to slit the throats of women and children. As usual, he drove looking over his shoulder.

"So what's happening?"

I brought him up to speed.

"Sounds like everything is going well," he remarked with satisfaction.

"I need a gun with a silencer."

"For who?"

"Ciccio Formaggio and the inside guy."

"The bodies?"

"Flambéed."

"What about the widow?"

That fucking cop knew where I was living. A way of letting me know I'd better not try to screw him. I took it without flinching. "A natural death. A sob story about loneliness."

He chuckled. "I found an abandoned house in the open countryside," he said, turning serious again. "It meets our needs. Nobody'll hear the shots, and it won't be necessary to dig graves. There's an old cistern to dispose of the bodies. We'll go and check it out the day after tomorrow. I'll bring the weapons." He pulled over to the sidewalk. There was nothing more to say.

Wednesday 11:00

Blazing sun. Been a while since I'd seen an October like this. At the old farm the roofs to the stables and barn had caved in long ago. But the house was fairly intact. Doors and windows torn out. Walls covered with graffiti. Signs of camping. A gutted mattress. Anedda pulled a satchel from the car and led me to the kitchen. It was roomy. A huge fireplace blackened by smoke and time and a sink of worn stone. In the center an ancient wooden table.

"I put that there. Found it upstairs." Then he began to explain his plan: "When you arrive, it'll be pitch dark. Get out of the car, shine a flashlight on the door and the hallway and lead them here. Switch on the camping light and tell the Spaniards to put the bags on the table. I'll be hidden outside the window. As soon as the money's on the table, I'll start shooting."

I looked over the scene. "I'll be in the middle of the crossfire."

"No, you won't," answered the cop. "But you'll have to be ready to duck behind the left side of the fireplace. You'll be covered, so you can shoot without getting into a panic."

The old stone structure was more than a meter deep and slightly less than a meter and a half high. Better than nothing. I spotted a shelf in the corner against the wall. A good hiding place for the shotgun I saved from the Kosovars at Mestre. I removed the rags I'd wrapped it in, checked to see it was loaded, and laid it on the shelf. It was the right weapon to use indoors. Impossible to miss the mark at close range.

"You need ammo?"

I shook my head. "Won't have time to reload."

Anedda opened the canvas bag. Pulled out a pump rifle with a collapsible stock, two high-caliber revolvers, and a .22 caliber semiautomatic with a silencer. An execution-style weapon. Killers once snubbed it because of its weak stopping power. Then the American mafia started using it with good results, and it became the thing. I picked it up to get a feel for it. The clip was loaded with full-metal-jacket bullets.

"Where'd they come from?"

"A souvenir of a search," he answered with a smile. "When you're a cop, you get into the wholesome habit of taking mementoes. Terrorists always had plenty of them."

He handed me one of the revolvers: a .357 magnum, Spanish make. "Put it next to the shotgun. It might come in handy."

I covered the weapons with a rag and again ran my eyes over the room, memorizing details. Then I followed the cop to the rear of the house. He slid back an old iron lid eaten by rust. I looked down. The bottom of the cement cistern was covered by a couple fingers of rainwater. That enormous grave would hide the bodies of our five accomplices.

"We'll dump them here."

"We can't," I objected. "Within four or five days the rotting corpses will have this whole place stinking to high heaven. All the fields around here are cultivated."

"We'll throw some wooden planks on the lid and cover it with dirt. They'll rest in peace for a good stretch."

Wednesday 19:00

"The nifty thing about this city is cocktail hour," said Ciccio Formaggio as he entered the bar. "The counters are packed with all kinds of goodies, and you might as well skip dinner."

"Did you get the cars?" I asked, heading for a table that was set apart from the rest.

"Yep. An Escort station wagon and a Renault 21. Makes that don't attract attention."

"They're not wrecks, I hope."

"No." He sounded certain. "I've driven them, and they handle like a dream. But just to be on the safe side I changed the oil, the filter and the plugs, checked the tires and filled the tank."

"Bravissimo!" I complimented him, smiling.

"I'm a pro," the idiot responded, pleased with himself.

"When will you take them to the garages?"

"Friday, late morning. The cops often make the rounds, hunting for stolen cars. At this point even they know the trick."

The waiter brought us two Negroni and a plate filled with tidbits. "You don't want any?" Ciccio asked in amazement, stuffing his mouth with peanuts. I didn't answer. He really was a greedy dimwit. I resumed talking about the hit. Told him the name of a bar in Porta Romana where he'd give me the garage receipts.

"Come with the inside guy. I want to look him in the face before we meet again to split the cash."

The ex-terrorist shifted uncomfortably in his chair. "Look, this is just what I wanted to talk about. The guard that tipped me on the heist doesn't want anybody to see him. Not even to take his share. He wants me to bring it to him."

I grinned. "Your buddy's trying to pull a fast one. If the police get suspicious and grill him, he can always say he talked to you, and you, the ex-con, took advantage of his good faith and organized the robbery. His word against yours. He'll stash the money somewhere, you'll end up in jail, and then he'll have a high old time."

Ciccio Formaggio stared at me. He was visibly racked with doubt.

"You think he wants to fuck me? Because you know, I'd stick him in a second, right in the belly," he whispered in a punchy tone.

I placed a hand on his arm. Like a real friend. "He won't be able to fuck anybody if he meets all of us. If we know who he is, we can always get revenge, even if it means confessing his role in the crime."

He still wasn't convinced. Against my better judgment I was

forced to reveal part of the plan. "We'll have to cover our asses and take out two of his co-workers. This security firm is going to be turned inside out like a sock. You do realize we have to grab him by the balls so his nerves don't get to him."

Ciccio nodded. "Shit, two killed," he said in a low voice. "I'll see he shows up at the meeting. Don't worry."

Friday 19:30

The inside guy was a big kid just under thirty. As I suspected, he had as much brains as Ciccio Formaggio. He thought he was entitled to some of the wealth he protected daily for a starvation wage. He ventured to the fringes of the criminal underworld because he knew honesty would guarantee him a skinny pension, at the most. But now he wanted to pull back. The time had ended for shooting the breeze and whispering secrets in the bar, where it seems easy enough to grab life by the throat. Now the thing was for real, and the money took on a slightly different color. It could buy the cars and women that had always been beyond his reach, but it could also lead straight to jail. And security guards, even if they took the plunge, were never popular.

I read all this in his eyes. Eliminating him had become a necessity. In front of the first cop who asked him the simplest question, he'd spill his guts. Another loser.

I acted nice. Dealt out winks, slaps on the back. The inside guy was called Ausonio. That night I probably killed the last dude who bore that name. I offered them a drink. Only one round. I was in a hurry to finish up because I really wanted to kill them. I felt the weight of the gun in one of my jacket pockets. In the other I kept the silencer. I spent the afternoon practicing so I could screw it on fast. I'd count to five and be ready to fire. The guard unbuttoned his cheap leather. A bulge in his sweater showed he had a gun in his belt. He wouldn't even have time to think about using it.

"Here are the keys and the garage receipts," said Ciccio as he passed me an envelope.

"Did you come by car?" I asked in a chatty tone.

"In his," answered Ciccio, pointing his thumb at his partner.

"Perfect," I said. "I'll take you to see the place where we'll meet to split the cash."

"Do I really have to come?" Ausonio stammered timidly.

I spread my arms. "Nobody's forcing you. But if you don't, the hit's off, and my partners'll be sore as hell at you. They'll think you've made us waste time and money, and they'll want to teach you a lesson."

The kid turned pale and bowed his head to his chest. He was starting to go bald and had a case of dandruff that hadn't been treated right. "I don't travel in your circles, and there are certain things I don't know."

"It's true," Ciccio intervened in his defense. "You've got to be patient with him. He ain't one of us."

"Now he knows the rules." I cut him short.

"OK," the guard blurted, "I'll go in all the way."

I stood up. "Follow me."

I got into my Panda. They took Ausonio's Tipo. I led them into the country, outside Cusago. Turned down a dirt road and drove within fifty meters of the abandoned house. Slipped on a pair of leather gloves. Climbed out of my car and got into theirs. I sat in the middle of the back seat.

"That's the place," I said as I took out the gun and the silencer. "Don't turn up before eleven tomorrow night. Signal you're here by flashing your high beams three times."

They were concentrating on my words as they looked at the house. I took off the safety, raised my arm and shot Ausonio in the head. Blood sprayed across the windshield. I shifted the weapon to the head of the dope, Ciccio Formaggio. Pulled the trigger. Another spray of blood. The silencer effectively muffled the shots. The ejected shells clinked against the window on my right. The car was filled with the smell of cordite and the sudden silence of death.

To avoid leaving any trace I had to gather the shells and stow the gun. I also had to remove the guard's semiautomatic, take the can of gas from my car, set the fire and slip away fast. I had no time to lose. Every second you spend at a crime scene for no reason is pure folly. I was aware of it, yet I calmly took my cigarettes and lighter from a trouser pocket. And smoked. An entire cigarette. I stretched out an arm and switched on the light inside the car. Took their wallets and poked around their lives. ID's, cards, photos. Ausonio smiling between two elderly people: Mamma and Papà. I abruptly ripped it in half. Ten minutes later I lit a second cigarette. Two drags, then I tossed it into the gas-soaked interior.

Saturday 11:30

The Spaniards were always late. They came in the bar with their hands thrust into their pockets. Pepe went to the counter and ordered a spremuta, freshly squeezed orange juice. Javier headed towards my table. I handed over the car keys and the receipt. He left in silence. His comrade paid for the drink. On his way out, he limited himself to a vacant glance in my direction.

Saturday 14:00

Another bar, another neighborhood. Romo Dujc, alias Cerni, was sipping a soft drink. Never anything alcoholic before laying your eye on the barrel of a precision rifle and pulling the trigger. Tonci Zaninovic, his partner, sat at another table, his eyes fixed on the street.

I tossed the envelope on the table. "Keys and receipt."

The Croat nodded. That day nobody wanted to talk.

Saturday 20:32

After the robbery I managed to reconstruct the facts from the newspapers and the eyewitness interviews aired by Lombard and national channels.

The armored truck arrived punctually at eight-thirty in the evening. The security guards spent two minutes checking the surrounding area. Then the driver and another guard climbed out, opened the steel door and removed the money bags. At that moment, they were cut down by a number of shots. Gianni Casiraghi, the driver, 41, separated with two daughters, was hit square in the face and in the throat. Walter Salemme, 29, married with a four-month-old baby, was hit in the temple. He died before he reached the ground. A Renault 21 pulled out from a row in the parking lot, speeding towards the spot where the bags had been left. Eyewitnesses were certain a woman was behind the wheel. In the meantime the shooters continued to fire at the rear door of the truck to prevent the other guard from returning the shots. But their effort was pointless. Antonio Donati, 33, married with no children, seeing his co-workers shot with lethal precision, lay flat on the floor of the truck, praying and sobbing. Terror had simply stopped him from seizing the radio microphone and sounding an alarm at the central office of the security firm. Two men got out of the Renault. One gathered the four bags; the other covered him, holding two guns. The newspapers had a field day, offering their readers computer-drawn diagrams and implausible hypotheses. The only accurate conjecture said it was likely the gang included an inside man. Ciccio and Ausonio had already been discovered, but car and bodies had been burnt so badly it would take time to determine their identities. The robbery made front-page news for several days, not only because of the two deaths, the funerals attended by high-ranking prelates, and the city in mourning, but also because of the size of the haul: eight hundred and seventy-five thousand euros. Unlike the usual drill, the authorities released only vague statements of little interest. The dynamic of the robbery and the discovery of some twenty Russian-made shells on the roof immediately put them on the trail of a dangerous foreign gang. A difficult investigation, where every detail could prove useful only if it wasn't made public.

Saturday 21:15

The gas station closed at 19:30. I parked the Panda behind the self-service car wash so I wasn't seen by the local cops. My presence could've aroused the curiosity of some passing patrol. The Croats' Escort arrived, followed closely by the Spaniards' Renault. I turned the key in the ignition and led them to the house. I was happy. Happy and excited by the idea of becoming rich. The last task would be dropping the bodies of my accomplices down the old cistern.

Saturday 22:40

To avoid roadblocks we were forced to travel back roads, often dirt tracks. I parked the car, turned on a powerful flashlight and signaled the others to follow me. The abandoned house was immersed in darkness. For a moment no one moved. The place seemed designed for a trap. Then everybody slipped their hands into their pockets, and the feel of their guns convinced them to go inside the house. In the kitchen I switched on the camping light. As I told the Spaniards to put the money on the table, I began moving towards my stash in the corner of the fireplace.

Anedda started shooting too soon and screwed everything up. He hit Pepe in the chest, killing him instantly; another round ripped Javier's side. But Francisca and the Croats still hadn't entered the room. They pulled back along the hallway, moving out of range. I grabbed the shotgun and slowly inched through the doorway, ready to shoot. But I was greeted by crossfire and had to take cover. Javier began to moan faintly. I took a gun and finished him off.

"You've really made a mess," I growled at Anedda, who'd entered through the window.

"We've got the money," he snapped, pointing at the bags on the table. "Let's go out and finish the job," he added, switching off the light.

But we were trapped in the room. The Croats had gone to the car to get their rifles with the infrared scopes, and protected by the darkness they kept us under fire. We couldn't see them.

"They've got us fucked."

"Let's deal."

"Don't waste your time trying to shoot us," I shouted. "We'll give you half the money, and everybody goes his own way."

"All the money," the Croat shouted back. "You're in no position to deal."

"We can hold out till dawn, and then you can pound your gunsights up your ass."

No answer. They were obviously considering the situation.

"What about the Spanish broad?" Anedda asked me.

Right. Francisca. "I have no idea," I answered. "Either the Croats snuffed her or she's hiding somewhere."

"What do we do?"

"The only thing we can do is stay covered. You keep an eye on the door; I'll watch the window."

We were interrupted by Romo's voice. "It's a deal. Throw out two bags, and we'll leave."

"Real smart, pal," Ferruccio remarked acidly.

"If you keep talking bullshit," I shouted, "we'll just get some shut-eye till morning. The money for the rifles with the scopes. And cut the crap."

"OK."

Another ten minutes passed before we reached an agreement on the exchange process. In the end, two bags and two

Dragunovs lay in the clearing in front of the house. Only then did I turn on the flashlight again. The blade of light cut through the darkness, and I could make out Romo and Tonci taking cover behind a car. But they weren't alone. Cerni was pulling Francisca by the hair, holding a knife to her throat. His partner, pistol in hand, kept firing at us. Anedda in turn had him lined up in the sight of the pump rifle.

The Croat sneered. "You head out. We're going to stay and have some fun with the anarchist whore."

With a jerk of her head Francisca tried to slit her own throat. She wasn't successful. Bad luck. Romo smacked her head against the car, and she slipped to the ground, out cold. The two Ustashi would have their own method of reviving her.

"What do we do?" I whispered to Ferruccio.

He shrugged. "The Spanish broad has to die anyway. While they're amusing themselves with her, we'll find a way to fuck them. Those two bags are ours."

"You've got a plan?"

"No, but I've got an idea: let's go have a chat with Luana."

"Perfect. You can bet she knows the assholes' next move."

"So what are you going to do?" the Croat pushed us.

"Alright, we're splitting," I said in a loud voice. "But the bodies can't be left out in the open. Before you take off, you have to hide them in the cistern at the back of the house."

"No problem," said Cerni.

"Now move away from the cars," I ordered.

While the cop covered my back, I climbed into the Panda and punched it in reverse till I pulled up right beside him. He got in. Then I shifted to first and floored it.

Sunday 01:25
Luana worked via Novara, in the San Siro area. But that night nobody had seen her.

"She's home," I suggested for the umpteenth time.

We were in Anedda's car. He could always flash his badge, but I didn't exactly feel relaxed, armed to the teeth with two bags of stolen cash in the trunk. He didn't give a fuck. He felt untouchable. He drove slowly, eyeballing the sidewalk crowded with whores from eastern Europe. That was their territory.

"She's got to be home waiting for the other two," I repeated one more time.

"OK, let's go see. But I'd prefer to pick her up on the street."

Twenty minutes later I was about to push the bell to her apartment. The cop stopped me with a wave. He took a step back and kicked in the lock. The door was shit. The wood gave with a crack. He went inside holding his pistol with two hands, in a shooting position. I followed him and drew my revolver. Luana Bazov, refugee from Vukovar, was in the bedroom packing her bags. When she saw us, her face became a mask of fear.

"Hurt her," my partner ordered.

I didn't have to be told. I faked a punch in her face, forcing her to protect herself by holding out her arms towards me. Then I grabbed one of her fingers and with a rapid twist snapped it. She lost her breath. I threw her on the bed. Ferruccio pushed the pistol into her left tit, right at her heart.

"Live whore, dead whore. Which game you want to play?"

"Live whore," the girl whimpered.

"We want Romo and Tonci."

"I don't know where they are," she answered, desperate.

"Dead whore," snarled the cop, lifting the gun barrel.

She was more afraid of her compatriots than our death threats. The Ustashi and their friends could hurt her family.

I bent over her. "If you help us find them, we'll kill them. You'll never see them again, and nobody'd link you to their deaths."

"You tell me the truth? You really kill that pig Romo?"

I'd guessed right. Gave her a complicit smile: "You bet."

Luana got her color back, sat up and told us she was supposed to wait for them at another apartment rented a few days ago. It'd serve as a hideout till the dust settled. Then a train to Genoa and a ship straight to Paraguay. Cerni decided she was his woman and she had to follow him wherever he went. But she hated him. She gave us the address and the keys and explained the signal they'd use with the doorbell. A short ring followed by two long ones.

"Disappear from Milano," Anedda warned her. "If I meet you again, you're dead."

I pointed at the bitch. "We're leaving behind a witness?"

He looked at her. "The last thing she'll want to do is talk about this business."

"She could tip the two Croats."

He shook his head. "She won't."

I shrugged. "I think it's an unnecessary risk. But you're the boss."

As we left the room, I turned towards her: "Since you're still alive, put some ice on your finger and go to an emergency room."

She burst into tears from the sheer relief of being spared by fate. Ferruccio the bull smiled, pleased with his grand gesture. Fact is, it was really stupid. Never trust a whore. But I didn't dare give him any back talk. A waste of breath. He wouldn't have changed his mind.

"Let's get a move on," said Ferruccio once we were in the car. "We have to arrive before them."

"How are we going to whack them in the apartment? We can't allow ourselves the luxury of a shoot-out."

"You have that pistol with the silencer?"

"It's at the widow's house. I wasn't planning to use it today."

"Then we'll just have to make do."

We parked a few blocks away and walked to the building, keeping our eyes peeled, checking out the parked cars. We didn't spot the Renault or the Escort. I rang the bell according to the signal. A minute later we entered the apartment with our weapons drawn. Empty. Apart from the Ustashis' bags. We quickly ransacked them. Clothes, three pistols, some boxes of ammo.

Anedda pointed to one box that contained the same kind of bullets used to murder the security guards. "When I find them, searching the apartment with my men, I'll be able to declare with absolute certainty that the two bodies belong to the marksmen. This will definitely give a boost to my career," he snickered, rubbing his hands together.

I looked at him in amazement. "You've got balls. How will you 'discover' the hideout?"

"The classic tip from an informer."

"What else? You cops use that excuse to justify everything."

"Stop bellyaching about the profession. Instead think how the investigation will pick up the Croats' trail—and we won't run any risks." He looked at his watch. "Our friends have probably finished messing around with the Spanish broad, and they'll be here any minute. Let's get ready to welcome them."

In the kitchen he turned over a wooden table and broke off a leg. "We'll use the Rwanda system. Rapid, silent and lethal."

Twenty minutes later the bell rang three times. I let them in. Romo entered first, followed by Tonci. Their hands were occupied with the rifles and money bags. The barrels of our guns were suddenly resting on their necks.

"On your knees. Hands behind your heads," ordered Anedda.

Romo obeyed. His buddy didn't need a translation. I left them no time to reflect. I put down the gun, grabbed the table leg and swung it with all my might against Cerni's skull. Raised it again over my head and hit Tonci Zaninovic. Then I stepped back to contemplate the scene: two bodies on the floor, skulls cracked, spots of blood on the wall, my shoes, Anedda's trousers.

The cop bent down to check the carotid. "They're still alive."

I cursed between my teeth. Rummaged through their bags. Returned with a bathrobe belt and pajama pants.

"Take care of the other one," I said, wrapping the pajama leg around Romo's neck.

You should never leave a crime scene in too much of a hurry. You risk overlooking some detail which could point the investigation in the right direction. Anedda and I fished through the dead men's wardrobe and changed our shoes and trousers. Our own clothes, along with the belt, pajama pants and table leg, wound up in a trash bag we later tossed in another neighborhood. The cop began to look for traces. Of course, not the ones we wanted to be found. We'd worn gloves through the whole thing and didn't have to worry about fingerprints. But the soles of our shoes were distinctly visible on the floor. I looked for a bucket and rag and solved the problem. In the end, we left satisfied. Anedda would return the next night, wearing a blue jacket with "Polizia" written on the back.

I still didn't know whether I could trust him. We were now the only ones left to split the cash. At any point he might be tempted to take it all. When we got into the car, I slipped my hand in my pocket, searching for my gun. He caught the move, but pretended he didn't.

"When do you think you'll kill the widow?" he asked.

"Tuesday, before I leave Milano."

"It might be too soon. Tomorrow I'm back on the job, and I'll see which way the wind blows. Wait for my call before you act."

"OK."

"You take the money. We'll split it before you leave. As soon as you've taken care of your host."

I swallowed hard. "You joking?"

"No. I can trust you because you wouldn't dream of fucking me. You just can't do it." He was right. He'd find me anywhere. "Count it and split it in half," he added. "Throw away the bags and put the cash in two travel bags."

The widow's apartment was sunk in silence. As always. When the television wasn't on, it seemed as if nobody was there. The phone never rang, the cell rarely. Calls from old johns worried they hadn't run into her in some hotel. The woman's solitude was chilling, and solitude was the only aspect of living that frightened me. When you're alone and lack the wherewithal, you're prey to somebody else. As she was to me. But that wouldn't happen to me: I'd organize my life differently and never be in her situation when I was up in years. That stupid broad didn't know how to look ahead, and she played her cards badly, acting out the role of the crime boss's widow for too long. But people forget fast, and she fell lower and lower, till she met me, sinking forever in the depths of defeat. All she lacked was a violent, unjust death, and I'd provide that very soon. I went to my room and threw money bags, pistol and shotgun on the bed. I sensed her presence at my back. I turned slowly and found myself staring into the eyes of the mistress of the house. She was wearing a black suit, sheer stockings, patent-leather shoes with high heels. Her hair was gathered into a simple chignon, and she was made up to perfection. For the first time she seemed like a real lady instead of some old whore.

"Are you going out?" I asked.

She shook her head and pointed to the bags. "I saw it on TV. From the beginning I knew you were setting up some hit, and I was only an inconvenient witness." She adjusted the cuffs of her silk shirt. "Once I was an elegant woman, and I want to die elegant."

I kept staring at her without saying a word. My silence confirmed her suspicions, but there was no point in reassuring her. If she hadn't taken off, it only meant she was ready to die, and I was the one to kill her.

"Don't worry. It won't happen tonight."

The widow nodded. She sat on the edge of the bed, crossed her legs and lit a cigarette. She ran her hand slowly over the bags. "When my man was alive, he used to let me count the money from robberies. He'd want me to paint my nails with a dark red polish from Chanel. Then he'd sit in an armchair and watch me handle the stacks of banknotes. After I finished, we would make love. And while he was in me, he would sniff my hands. They smelled like money. Then he got important and sent others to knock over the banks. He increased the volume of his business, drugs, gambling, money-laundering, and from then on he began to have other women. I used to stroll through Milano in furs and jewels, like a princess, but at night I slept alone. I never stopped loving him, but I'm the kind of woman who loves one man in her life, and when they killed him, I became 'the widow.' Forever."

I remembered it. The boss was in the courtyard of the maximum-security prison at Cuneo when a group of killers hired by the Cutolo family surrounded him and stabbed him to death. He was so despised they ripped his heart out and threw it in the dirt.

"After the funeral," the woman resumed her melancholy tale, "some of the new bosses courted me for a while. But only for the pleasure of screwing the old boss's wife. An insult without any risks, the sort of thing cowards do. I preferred to defend his memory and fuck up my life. Then you arrived. You made me realize how humiliating it is to keep on living like this. I'm not afraid of dying anymore; my grave has been ready for so long. Next to my man. I want only two things from you: don't let me suffer too much and let me be found elegant, as I am now. I don't want the newspapers to say I went out like a bag lady."

I smiled at her. "Relax. You'll look smart," I lied. My plan anticipated something very different for her. I changed the subject: "I'm tired. Count the money, and divide it into two piles."

"There aren't many of you left to split the take. True men of honor."

I slipped into the shower to wash away the stench of death and fear that seeped into my clothes and brain. I started to relax and felt glad. Didn't take long to realize I'd become a millionaire. Not bad for somebody who'd left Central America with a life sentence on his back. Finally I was rich, and I could think of building the life that was my due, after so much hard work. Even the widow's resigned attitude added to my satisfaction. I had no desire for any more trouble. When I returned to the room, she was still counting. I went into the parlor, poured myself a drink and switched on the TV. Every channel was showing special reports on the robbery of the superstore. The images were nearly always the same: the bodies of the two guards covered with a sheet and the men from forensics carrying out the investigation. I raised my glass to toast my plan. Simple, easy and therefore brilliant.

The widow came over to me. "Eight hundred seventy-five thousand. Congratulations." Then she looked at the images that flew across the screen. "Once the underworld would give part of the money to the widows. Even the cops' widows."

"Don't talk crap. These are tales your boss told you to make you think he was a great man," I scowled back at her. "Get lost. Go to your room."

That night I slept with the pistol under my pillow. I was rational enough to know I was safe, but it was difficult to manage the tension, and I awoke at the slightest sound. In the morning I opened my eyes and found the widow sitting on the bed in her dressing gown. She was wearing her hair loose on her shoulders, and she smelled sweet and clean. She lit a cigarette and started telling anecdotes about when she was still somebody. A real pain in the balls. I wanted to send her away, but it was better to let her chill. She'd create fewer problems when she quit life on earth. Every so often I nodded, feigning interest. But as she spoke, my mind was far away, back in that town, back with Flora. For a few minutes I let myself go with a dream beyond my reach: getting her back through the persuasive power of money. When I recalled the fucks in the rear of the shoe store, my cock got hard as marble. I took the widow's hand and slipped it under the covers. "Make yourself useful," I told her.

Time stopped, and the wait for Anedda's call became aggravating. The widow began to lose control of her nerves. She alternated between moments of apparent calm and crying jags. The TV was constantly tuned into the news programs. One night I caught my partner showing off at a press conference to report the discovery of "the robbers' hideout, along with two of them dead, probably Croatian extremists." I switched it off. No need to follow the news to see if the investigation had made any progress. Everything was under control.

I packed my bags. The ones with the money and the ones with my clothes. Monday my cell phone rang.

"Tomorrow morning they're taking down the road blocks," Anedda quickly announced. "At ten on the dot be at the restaurant where we ate together." Then he laughed and added: "With my bag, of course."

The widow, however, was sobbing. In silence but uncontrollably. Her eyes were red and puffy.

I put my arm around her shoulders. "You might feel better if you took a nice hot bath. It'll relax you."

I helped her undress and fill the tub with water, salts and bubble bath. Then I filled the baby bottle with Fernet and grabbed the sleeping pills. When she saw me coming back, she was terrified.

"I'm leaving in three days," I lied to calm her down.

I put the nipple in her mouth and rattled off an unlikely string of empty but sentimental words. She sucked the bottle to the last drop, like a good baby. Twenty-five minutes later she passed out. I took her feet, slipped them under my armpits, and grasping her firmly by the knees began to slide her head into the water. The survival instinct drove her to make a few convulsive movements in an effort to re-emerge, but they were weak and didn't amount to much. When I was sure she was dead, I rearranged her body in the tub.

Then I started to clean the apartment, removing traces of my presence as well as my prints. As I combed through the rooms, I made the most of it by searching for things that might be worth snatching. Lucky I did: I learned the old whore had tried to screw me. Hidden in a drawer I found an envelope with the line, "To be read after my death." Inside were a couple pages scrawled with handwriting that was shaky but completely legible. In the wrong hands they'd cost me a life sentence. I was trembling like a leaf. A panic attack drove me to turn the place upside down twice. The next morning on my way out, still stressed by the idea the widow had hidden other letters, I was hit with the urge to torch everything. I managed to calm down and convince myself that if I didn't run across them, then the cops wouldn't either. I finally found the strength to open the door and leave. I decided not to say a word to Anedda. Any suspicion about my involvement might make him think I was a potential threat. And shoot me in the head.

Ferruccio the bull arrived in an unmarked police car. I opened the door and laid a bag on the seat. His share of the loot. He shifted gears and took off, saying goodbye with a hurried wave. I followed the car with my eyes till it got lost in traffic. I was thinking I did the right thing to trust a cop who was elegant outside but rotten inside. I'd later kick myself for it. What's more, being unable to know or imagine it then would never turn into a good excuse. With a caper like that, another corpse wouldn't have made the slightest difference. Simply because you can never trust a cop. They're like whores, always asking you for one last favor. The favor that fucks you. Instead of dropping the bag in the car, I should've pulled the pistol with the silencer. Three, four shots would've taken care of everything forever. Then there'd be no split with anybody. My mistake was thinking a cop I did business with could always come in handy. As soon as I stopped playing cops and robbers and entered the real world, I realized cops didn't count for shit. There was an underworld of "professionals," each one with his specialty, his contacts, his terms and his hefty price tag. They were the ones who'd solve your problems. And they couldn't give a fuck about the law or the police.

I got into my Panda. It was transporting more than half a million in different denominations, all flying the flag of the European Union. I turned onto the highway heading northeast. I still wasn't clear about my future, but I knew I was moving in the right direction, where anybody who had balls and brains could go far: the northeast that belonged to the winners.

LA NENA

A FEW DAYS AFTER I turned forty-one, I settled in a town in Veneto. Which one really doesn't matter. Padova, Treviso, Vicenza—the hunger for money was the same everywhere. The choice, however, wasn't casual. I moved to where the lawyer Sante Brianese lived, the professional who was going to be my ticket to the world of honest citizens. I came across his name in San Vittore: he was recommended by a former bank manager convicted of fraud and embezzlement. Just in case I ever needed a shyster.

"He doesn't know shit from shinola when it comes to criminal proceedings," the man made clear. "But he's able to solve the myriad problems that result from a criminal case, particularly the investment of capital from illegal sources." In the beginning I had no intention of turning to him. I thought about managing on my own. But very soon I was forced to realize my act wasn't together, not even to rent an apartment, and every time I got stopped at a road block, my criminal past caused me endless headaches.

Brianese received me in an office that wasn't flashy, fitted out with simple but expensive furnishings. His height was average, but he had a trimness that came from regular trips to the tennis court. An elegant man who inspired trust. The angular lines of his face made him resemble a nineteenth-century broker, giving the impression he could solve any problem whatsoever. When I mentioned where I met the person who recommended him, he told me to put an advance against his fee on the desk.

"Fine," he said, slipping the banknotes into his jacket. "Now, sir, you are my client. Speak as freely as you wish."

Actually I got straight to the point. I limited myself to sketching my situation: an ex-con with a certain amount of capital to invest in the restaurant business.

"Come back tomorrow at the same time," the lawyer dismissed me. "Your explanation of your predicament was crystal clear. Nonetheless, you do understand I must make the necessary inquiries."

"Your problem, sir, is called rehabilitation," he began to explain the next day. "Our penal code contains the provision that a convict, after giving proof of spotless conduct for five years, may petition a surveillance judge to regain his civil rights. In short, the acceptance of this petition removes the stigma of being a previous offender."

"And then everything becomes easier," I observed.

The lawyer smiled. "Yes, precisely. From what I gather, you finished serving your sentence around three years ago—"

"Three years and two months."

"Within a couple years, therefore, we shall be able to present a petition of rehabilitation, provided your demeanor following your prison release has kept within the bounds of the utmost legality."

I shifted uncomfortably in my chair. "Well, for a time I worked at a lap-dancing joint. Police, carabinieri and revenue officers would often pay us a visit, and my name must turn up in their reports, especially since my employer went to jail for drug dealing."

"Were you directly involved in the investigation?"

"No."

"Then we have nothing to worry about. The important thing is that, starting now, you must avoid traveling in circles that are not above reproach. I am already convinced you are doing this if, from what I gather, your intention is to invest in a restaurant, a profitable activity that is completely respectable."

"Exactly. I have at my disposal a certain amount, and my goal is to open a decent place."

"How much?"

"Half a million."

"The savings of a lifetime," joked the lawyer. "Around here it isn't important to know where the money originates," he added, turning serious again. "But it mustn't stink of wrongdoing. On the contrary, it should carry the fragrance of hard work and a creative intellect. You understand what I mean?"

"Perfectly. This is precisely why I have turned to you."

"You have done well. Follow my instructions, and I guarantee you shall obtain what you wish."

The first instruction involved his fee. For his feasibility study he demanded ten thousand, in cash. Before dismissing me he asked where I was living. I gave him the name of a hotel on the outskirts. The lawyer was shocked.

"The police have the hotels in that area under constant surveillance," he scolded me, shaking his head. "If they discover that you are unemployed, you risk an expulsion order."

He took a pair of keys from a drawer. "A friend of mine owns a pied-à-terre in the centro. Small but comfortable."

I reached out a hand. "How much?" I asked.

"One thousand a month."

The lawyer was telling the truth. The small apartment was tastefully furnished. And the view over the roofs of churches and ancient palazzos was enchanting. A glance at the bathroom and the fridge was enough to tell me nobody ever lived there. The place was a love nest. Probably belonged to the lawyer himself, who took his lady friends there and staged his little orgies. I moved in, bringing only the suitcases filled with money and the pistol with the silencer. Dumped my clothes the day before. Decided to change my look and finally get my clothes from a tailor. Like somebody with self-respect. I also went to a beauty salon. While I was waiting my turn to get a manicure, I flipped through some magazines without paying much attention. Found myself staring at a photo of the widow, when she was still young and smiling. The weekly had dedicated a three-page spread to her. I didn't waste time reading it. The title said it all: "Accident or Suicide?"

Some ten days later I walked into Brianese's office dolled up like a real gentleman. The lawyer gave me the once-over without a word. I took a seat and lit a cigarette.

"Good news," the lawyer began, examining a set of pages spread across the desk. "But before I explain my plan to you, I would like to discuss my fee."

"How much?" I was up front.

"One hundred and fifty thousand in monthly installments until you obtain the rehabilitation and ten percent of your profit for the next five years."

I stared at him, not buying it. The figure sounded steep. "What kind of guarantee are you offering?"

Brianese shrugged. "None. But the chances for success are reasonably good."

I could've threatened him. Promised him a bullet in the head if the thing flopped or, worse, if it turned out to be a rip-off. But the man wasn't stupid. He couldn't be unaware of the risks involved, and he certainly knew his business.

"OK, counselor. I'm listening."

La Nena was an old osteria downtown, run by an elderly couple. Toni and Nena. Once she'd been a knockout, turned heads, especially with loads of customers. Now past seventy, she couldn't wait to retire with her husband to a cottage in the country. Their two kids had studied at the university and didn't want to follow in their parents' footsteps. Brianese's plan had me starting off as a waiter at the osteria and gradually taking charge. Once rehabilitated, I'd become the owner, changing the place to suit myself. In the meantime I'd learn the trade by taking some specialized courses.

Toni and Nena had obviously agreed, and they already fixed the purchase price. Half when I began working, the rest when we closed the deal.

"We won't hide your past," the lawyer explained. "People are going to find out about it anyway, and that would make it worse. We'll present you as a decent guy, the victim of bad companions, ready to demonstrate the change in your behavior as well as your intrinsic worth. Your attitude must be unobtrusive but at the same time simpatico: you need to be well-liked. Above all, you must avoid any display of wealth. The clothes you're now wearing must be stored away till you become the owner. Shop for clothes at the big department stores, as every waiter does. Don't frequent expensive restaurants or cafés and certainly not nightclubs or lap-dancing joints. Your life must be home and work. I'll provide your clientele. Select and first-rate. In time we'll turn the osteria into an exclusive spot. I intend to enter politics, and La Nena could become my club."

"Politics? What kind of politics?"

"Moderate and destined to govern," he answered with a wink. "I represent a group of businessmen and professionals who have long been marginalized in the political life of this city. But now the wind has changed, and we intend to count more and more. Here and in Roma. You'll have the opportunity to make contacts that will prove useful as you become a seamless part of the urban fabric. What do you think?"

"The plan seems perfect," I answered, cautious.

"It *is*." He was offended. "Provided you don't ruin it by doing something foolish."

"I don't have the slightest intention of doing that."

Brianese changed the subject. "Since you'll be forced to

draw on your capital for my fee and the down payment on the osteria, I can direct you to a reliable person who will help you recoup part of the money."

"How?"

"Loans. Consistent, fast and profitable. If you have any ready money on hand, take advantage of this investment opportunity. It's good business."

The lawyer spoke for another hour. Instructions, advice, cautions. That guy in San Vittore was right. Sante Brianese was up on his stuff. He thought of everything. In a couple years I'd build a respectable position, putting my past behind me forever.

When I left the office, I was tempted to celebrate in a deluxe restaurant. But I remembered the lawyer's warnings and slipped into a self-service eatery that belonged to the Break chain. Then straight home.

In the days that followed I met several of Brianese's reliable people, those who would look after the fiscal end of the operation. I also became acquainted with the employment consultant who ran the loansharking scheme. A bank manager sent him clients who needed loans. The money was doled out by a financial institution that acted as a broker, providing credit and handling debt collection. The scheme was well put together. He tried to convince me I could trust him with a hundred and twenty-five grand, but in the end I gave him only thirty-five. I decided to keep something in reserve, just in case the deal went south and I was suddenly forced to go on the lam.

At last Brianese accompanied me to my restaurant. It was located beneath the porticoes of an old street, near Piazza del Mercato. Toni and Nena welcomed the lawyer with fearful reverence. They must've owed him a huge debt of gratitude. With me they limited themselves to a simple handshake. Toni had the look of a drinker at the end of a long night. But Nena was full of energy, still trying to act like the boss. They both wore blue smocks. I hadn't seen that since I was a kid. Even the regulars weren't young anymore. Apart from some groups of students and weirdoes with braids and face jewelry who I'd toss out at the first opportunity. The place—one large room scattered with tables and wooden chairs—smelled of reheated food, stale smoke and wine. A marble counter lined an entire wall. Opposite stood the bathroom and a door that opened onto an inner courtyard, which communicated with a storeroom packed with demijohns. Everywhere oil paintings done in the most different styles. For a while, it seems, Toni took in washed-up artists who paid for some meals with their work. Nena told me she and her husband came into the place as soon as the war ended. The Jews who ran it before were taken away by supporters of the Republic of Salò in '44. Since then nothing had changed. The same wine as always, the same menu. Stewed tripe, cod with polenta, braised beef, chicken cacciatore. On the counter lay plates of sliced calf's head, meatballs, vegetable omlets, hard-boiled eggs with pickles, grilled soppressata and boiled baby octopus. Brianese told me it was among the last of the old-fashioned osterias in Italy. A local group had in fact put it on a list of historical landmarks to be preserved. The lawyer had a very different idea. An architect friend of his was going to turn it into a trendy joint. Salmon-colored walls, French décor. They did have a point. The osteria definitely needed a good coat of paint.

I started washing dishes and waiting on tables. The place opened at seven in the morning and closed at eight in the evening. By the time I got home, I was done in. A shower, a plate of pasta, then I headed out for my lesson with the cavaliere Minozzi. For forty years he ran the best restaurant in the city— until gambling debts prevented him from paying his suppliers. The matter might've wound up in court, if Brianese hadn't intervened just in time to calm down the creditors. At that point, Minozzi's kids made him sell the place and withdraw into private life. He was a spry old man, who in exchange for his advice obliged me to play countless card games. I was a jail-house gambler, slick and light-fingered, and I took him for a ride. He was amused, and between hands he'd give me the best tips for my future occupation. His wife, a pretty little woman who fussed over us like a mother, made sure we were fortified with slices of torta and liqueurs. Minozzi proved to be an invaluable teacher. After a couple months I introduced the first two epoch-making changes in the history of La Nena. I elimi-nated the bulk wine and the old glasses. I substituted a selec-tion of bottles from the best vineyards in Veneto, Trentino and Friuli, in addition to some good reds from Piemonte and Toscana. And I replaced the Duralex glasses with goblets and flutes. Obviously prices rose, and pensioners were the first to search for another spot to drink their euro's worth of red wine. Toni and Nena cast silent looks of disapproval in my direction. To the old customers who asked for explanations, they could furnish only vague, long-faced replies. Toni just kept repeating, like a robot, "Times change. Things ain't what they used to be."

The next move was to spruce up the dishes on the counter. Cold cuts, tartines, sandwiches. These innovations, along with a thorough housecleaning, were enough to set going a gradual change in clientele. After the old people, the students and weir-does cleared out. For some time now the place was losing money, but luckily the cash I invested in the loans was more than enough to stop the leaks. Thanks to Brianese's word-of-mouth, the osteria started to draw a fashionable crowd. They'd show up at cocktail hour. Prosecco and finger food. Plus a flood of advice. Everybody had something to recommend. From wines to salads. Most of the time it was names I'd never heard of. It seemed as if people from a certain class were only con-cerned with money and what they stuffed in their mouths. I soon realized something had happened in this country. There'd been a change in taste. I set up a table for consulting specialized guides and magazines. Customers would constantly ask for them so they could show friends a review of a restaurant or an oak-aged wine. Everybody played gourmet. Toni and Nena didn't resist all these changes. No, they asked the lawyer if they could step aside earlier than the agreement stipulated. Brianese told them to spread the word they intended to sell out, and in the meantime I'd stand in for them. First off I hired a couple young guys to wait on tables. On the advice of an antique dealer, I dressed them like waiters in a Parisian brasserie. Despite all my efforts and the quality of the snacks and the wines, the place still remained an osteria. The weak point was the kitchen. The new clientele wasn't nostalgic for Nena's rich, oily dishes. Cavaliere Minozzi put together a light menu for me, with some pastas and a variety of salads. I found a young cook who'd just graduated from a school for the hotel trade, and in no time I was able to get a stream of customers to come regularly for lunch. I enrolled in a course for sommeliers as well as in every course organized by the various gourmet clubs and associations. I spent almost every evening at tastings and lectures in oenology, and frankly it was pleasurable.

After so many years hanging out with militants and guerrillas, pimps and thieves, I finally found myself among normal people. People who had an absolutely normal existence. They moved from school to university, from the start of a career to marriage. I envied them. This new life dedicated to work was so different from how I lived till the day I drowned the widow, that my memories grew more and more confused. I felt calmer, discovered new sensations and began to appreciate things that had always been uninteresting to me, like music and cinema. I liked different kinds of women. But I didn't know how to approach them. Blackmail and bullying wouldn't have worked. They belonged to another world. The rumors about my past, deliberately fed by Brianese, made the rounds of the city, but I didn't get wind of any negative comments. Curiosity, yes. Lots of it. Every so often somebody'd ask me a question about terrorism or jail. All of sudden you could hear a pin drop, and everybody was staring at me, waiting for the answer. The lawyer rehearsed me well on the topic, and with a melancholy smile stamped on my face, I told them what they wanted to hear. That circle included some former leftists. Often they'd draw close and, with a conspiratorial air, confide to me they once belonged to some left-wing revolutionary group. Youthful mistakes. The news of the final verdict in the Calabresi case was announced at the osteria by a lawyer who'd just returned from the court in Venezia. It was cocktail hour, and La Nena was packed. The conviction was greeted by satisfied shouts and even squeals of joy from a couple ladies. Sante Brianese organized a toast, and suddenly I found everybody's eyes pointed at me.

I understood what was at stake. "It's on me!" I shouted with pleasure, raising a bottle of prosecco. I searched the crowd for the ex-revolutionaries: they were all competing to show they'd burnt their bridges with the past. I smiled, pleased. I was in good company.

When I managed to keep the osteria open till one at night, there was a real jump in quality. I had to hire more personnel, but the stream of customers swelled to a river. I trusted one of the young guys I just hired to open the place in the morning: he'd shown himself to be serious and reliable. I arrived about eleven and took care of the closing. The clientele in the evening was completely different. Apart from a few people who also appeared during the day, the night crowd hung out exclusively after dinner. It didn't take me long to see they were all linked to Brianese. Either professionally or politically. Or both. I followed the advice of an interior decorator and got rid of the old

neon lights, replacing them with sconces that made the atmos-
phere more welcoming. At night, the place entirely lost the look
of an osteria. Wise old Minozzi drew up a menu of elegant
drinks that customers were delighted to quaff as they chatted
amiably at the tables. Brianese played the gracious host. He
moved from one table to another, cutting deals and widening
the circle of his supporters. His objectives were clear. Regional
councilman for one legislature, then straight to Palazzo
Montecitorio Parliament. I had no doubt about his success, and
many people thought just as I did, judging from the deference
they adopted towards this bigwig. In reality, he didn't give a
damn about politics. It was simply a tool to achieve his goals.
Which were illicit, for the most part. His field was white-collar
crime, purely financial. Fact is, thugs tied to drug trafficking or
prostitution never set foot in the osteria. Let alone trash from
outside the European Union. Even honest trash. Brianese had
grasped the economic model of the northeast, the famous
"locomotive" as the media called it: the legal and illegal
economies were merged in a single system, offering the opportunity to grow rich and build a discreet position of power. And
he milked it with intelligence and sound judgment. Business,
crime and politics. This new mafia was blazing the trail.

Brianese's closest collaborators included a number of former politicians and public administrators who got into trouble
with the Tangentopoli scandal. There was also a former com-
mander of the revenue police. He'd just finished serving a six-
year sentence for extortion and bribery. The judges were convinced he managed to stash away a huge fortune. For a time
they even conducted a search for it abroad, but they were
forced to give up. Brianese did an excellent job. Most of his
associates were active in center-right politics: they dreamed of
settling accounts not only with the judges who had them inves-
tigated, but with the political forces that supported the judges'
work. Others boasted of affiliations with the movement for

regional autonomy, but aside from some arguments the ambience was absolutely serene. The only unpleasant episode occurred, not quite because of politics, but because of music. On the first anniversary of Lucio Battisti's death, a group of customers, fans of the dead singer, planned an evening to remember him. They arrived with records and guitars. There were sing-alongs, some tears and lots of applause. At a certain point, this joker who spent the night drinking on his own came up to the bar. I'd never seen him before. He was tall, beefy, had blue eyes. And he was drunk. He waved me over.

"Battisti sang the platitudes of the Italian petty bourgeoisie," he said under his breath.

"You're in the wrong place to make a crack like that," I warned him.

"The lyrics are nothing but disgusting banalities, and the melodies—"

"If you cut it out, I'll give you a beer on the house."

"A toast to Fabrizio De Andrè," he boomed.

Then all hell broke loose. Battisti's fans started to insult him. Somebody shouted, "You fucking communist." And everybody wanted me to throw him out of the place. Signora Cardin, the owner of a beauty salon, tried to go for him. To settle the matter I had to sock the guy in the belly. Then I grabbed him by the scruff of the neck and dragged him away. Customers clapped, and I received a load of compliments and slaps on the back.

That night I got laid for the first time in my new life. Gianna, one of the regulars, had been giving me the eye for a while now. A pretty little brunette, about forty. According to the line I picked up from friends, her husband was neglecting her because of work. Officially he was known to be a craftsman in business for himself. In reality, he was the owner of a genuine firm that specialized in flooring. Completely unknown to the tax collector. Projects, resources, personnel were all managed off the books. Business was booming: you could see it from the jewels and furs the wife flaunted recklessly. She stayed to chat with me at the bar till closing time. I took her to the storeroom and slipped a hand under her skirt. She was hot and knew just what to do. It happened other times, always pleasurable.

Then I met Nicoletta. Blond, tall, slim, with huge milky-white tits. A chain smoker who loved aged reds, she dealt in haute couture and always wore elegant, expensive clothing. Hermès or Chanel. They formed part of her sample collection. The merchandise was strictly fake, but for many ladies of high society and a few shopkeepers, this detail could be overlooked. She'd already gone to court a few times, and the lawyer was always able to get her out of trouble. There was no need to lead her to the storeroom. She was separated and lived in a comfortable house in the suburbs. She'd drop in a couple nights each week, wait till I lowered the shutters and take me to her place.

Around then I decided to move out of the lawyer's love nest. I strolled into a real-estate agency in the centro, and the mention of La Nena was enough for security. I rented an apartment near the osteria. Nicoletta helped me furnish it. For the first time I felt a house belonged to me. Picking out furniture and other things with her, I got a taste of the pleasure to be had from sharing something with a woman. I began to desire a lasting relationship. With Gianna and Nicoletta there was nothing beyond physical attraction and hitting it off together. But for me it was something new. I felt no need to use them as a doormat and control their lives, as I did with Flora and the widow. Still, this didn't mean my sexual preferences had changed. I constantly experienced new sensations. And I liked that. Maybe this is what it means to turn a new leaf.

After exactly a year Brianese came to ask me for his first favor. The pay was tops, but the thing fell outside the deal we'd struck. A woman who sold housewares in the area had been swindled by a psychic. Shelled out over twenty-seven grand to cure her daughter from a serious case of anorexia. The lawyer wanted me to get it back.

"I've turned a new leaf." Full stop.

"Of course. And with excellent results. Except you have a wealth of experience that none of us possesses. It's only right that you enlist it in the service of your friends. You know quite well that some situations can't be resolved with a legal intervention."

"This means there'll be more favors?"

"Possibly. You've had enough time to look around and realize you can make a fortune here, living happily and calmly with the right sort of contacts. Contacts, however, must be cultivated—"

"The risks?"

"Minimal. Besides, this is about small fry. And remember you've got your ass covered."

"When you spoke to me about the rehabilitation, you told me to steer clear of certain circles and keep my conduct irreproachable—"

The lawyer cut me off with an impatient wave. "What's the problem?"

"I don't want to jeopardize the rehabilitation."

"It won't happen. You have my word."

I stared at him. I had absolutely no desire to risk everything I'd built with so much effort. But I owed it all to Sante Brianese, and I had to do what he wanted. Always. Obey him like a slave.

"OK."

The lawyer recovered his smile and good humor and, after an anecdote and some witty remarks, told me about the healer. The con game was simple. Jessica the fortune-teller publicized her magic powers through a local TV station. The housewares dealer, desperate because of her daughter's health, set up an appointment. For a hundred euros Jessica had the mother explain her worries, promising to consult the mysterious forces of the occult and verify the potential for solving the problem. She arranged another appointment to take place ten days later. In the meantime the healer followed her usual practice and hired a private investigator to gather as much information as he could about her client, especially her economic prospects. At the next meeting Jessica looked grim. Without mincing words she told the dealer her daughter was getting worse by the hour and only an esoteric intervention could save her. And so in the course of four sessions the client found herself relieved of a tidy sum. When her husband learned about what happened, he turned to the lawyer.

Jessica received her clients in quite a few northeastern towns. I set up an appointment in Mestre. I'd never been there, and nobody knew me. Some dude who looked like a disco bouncer showed me into the office. When he opened the door, I hit him with a sock filled with a few rolls of coins. Before he dropped to the floor, I pushed him into the room with all my might. He landed on the carpet right in front of Jessica's desk.

The woman jumped to her feet. "My God," she shouted, terrified.

I silenced her with a slap. I expected to find some weird chick, but she was just an overweight woman in a floral dress, about fifty, with teased hair and chubby hands full of rings. I grabbed her by the throat.

"You've got three days to give back the dealer's money."

She nodded. I felt I hadn't frightened her enough, so I broke her arm, like the Romanians did with me. The fortune-teller fainted. I would've threatened her again, but it was impossible to bring her around. So much the worse for her. When you go to collect a debt, you need to demonstrate you know no limits to violence. I punched her several times in the face, flattening her nose properly. Then I turned to deal with her bodyguard.

Kicked him a few times in the mouth and the balls. Neither of them would've talked to the cops. Jessica made the deadline for the restitution: three days later the dealer regained possession of her cash.

Brianese congratulated me and handed me an envelope with the compensation. I used it for a down payment on a car. The time had come to scrap the old Panda. I chose another compact. The pimpmobile was still a long ways off.

I was asked for more favors. But the lawyer always respected our agreement: they were no great shakes.

"Your role is to protect our group of friends from external aggression," he once told me. "To restore legality. Ours, of course."

In general, I had to flex some muscle. A few times I didn't even have to use violence. As in the case of a client who maintained a bank manager in the province had her sign blank fiduciary notes to guarantee a loan for a hundred-and-fifty thousand. I went no further than to advise her to withdraw the charge. On other occasions I was forced to be really nasty. As in the case of Alexia, a whore from Trieste who was blackmailing a devoted customer of La Nena. The guy, a well-to-do entrepreneur of metal trinkets, jewelry and what not, met the broad in a nightclub. Let himself be led back to her place for a boff to the tune of two-hundred-and-fifty euros. While they were in bed, a video camera hidden in a bookcase got the whole thing. To stop her from sending an anonymous package to the entrepreneur's wife and the two dailies in town, Alexia wanted a hundred grand.

I escorted the guy to the meeting arranged for handing over the cash. When the girl looked through the peephole, she saw only her client, but when she opened the door, she found me. Frightened, she tried to call the entrepreneur, who was heading for the stairs. I socked her in the pit of the stomach and pushed her inside. I recovered the cassette. But despite her squawks, I didn't believe her when she swore she made no copies. I tied her to a chair. From the kitchen I took a bag of coarse salt, a funnel and a carafe of water. A standard police interrogation. After the second carafe she came clean: there were two more cassettes in the wardrobe between the sheets. Alexia had decided to pluck her chicken but good. I told the entrepreneur other copies of the video existed and it'd cost him ten thousand to get them. He paid without any guff.

Once they told me to pull a robbery. Well-paid and, I imagine, commissioned by some pharmaceutical manufacturer. I had to sneak into a hospital ward and lift a few files that contained clinical data on the patients. Child's play.

The lawyer was also right on the issue of friends. When the customers realized I enjoyed his trust, they started treating me differently. Not like one of them, but like somebody they could do business with. This got me involved in a couple more loan-sharking rings. I became a partner in an illegal knitwear workshop that employed Chinese labor. Above all, I invested in quick, profitable deals, from lots of wine to furniture, from New Year's fireworks to computers. This is how things were in the northeast. A rapid turnover of goods and cash. You only needed to be in the right circle. And I was definitely in the right one.

Under the term "friends" I also listed a number of cops. Every kind, from carabinieri to traffic police. The ones that paid court to Brianese often hung out at La Nena. Others dropped by every once in a while to have a drink. In the beginning their presence gave me the jitters. Then I got used to them. The lawyer wasted no opportunity to praise my drive for reinstatement. In time they started to ask me questions about some of the customers. This came as no surprise. Most club owners are informers. Some guys got hassled thanks to my tips, which only had to do with penny-ante stuff. Fake screen tests, vacation scams, traffic in art works. All rigged by third-rate criminals. People in such a hurry to make money they take short cuts, thinking it'll be easy. So easy they allow themselves the luxury of running off at the mouth. I myself was more than happy to furnish information to the police. It served to pave the way for my reinstatement in society. Once even the Digos showed up. Right after the D'Antona murder. They asked me to let them know if I was contacted by any old comrades from the days of armed struggle.

"They'd never come to me."

"You never know. Everybody fucks up some time," the oldest cop was quick to answer.

"We're interested in the ones at the community centers," explained another.

"They don't hang here."

"True. But keep your ears open just the same. You got it?"

"I got it."

I was sure I was right. Everybody in town knew La Nena was run by an ex-terrorist. And the ones at the community centers also knew how I avoided the life sentence. They showed me by writing "Pellegrini infame" on the shutters "Pellegrini the Rat." More than once. I'd cover it with a coat of paint, and they'd come back with a spray can, fire-engine red. One night somebody wrote, "After Seattle no business as usual." I recognized the slogan. It was written on every wall in town. I didn't erase it. It didn't concern me.

Sante Brianese became regional councilman. After a skillful campaign he managed to win an aldermanship which guaranteed a good turnover. He celebrated at La Nena. Rivers of champagne, hugs from old friends, solemn handshakes from new ones. His court was growing bigger and bigger. The refreshments were on me. I was sincerely happy about his success. But also because I felt I now had the rehabilitation within my reach. The five-year waiting period would be over in four months. Then, after the petition was filed, I'd have to wait the usual time for the inquiry and for the date of the hearing to be set. Eight, ten months at the most. At forty-four I'd become a citizen to all intents and purposes. That night Brianese wrapped his arm around my shoulder.

"It's time you found yourself a nice girl," he said in a fatherly tone. "People are saying you're a skirt-chaser, and that's not good. Here we get married in church first. Then, with the priest's blessing, you screw every cunt that happens to come your way."

What he said made me think seriously about marriage for the first time. It was a good idea. Living with a woman could be useful and pleasurable. I started looking around. Very soon I spotted a woman around thirty-five who came to have lunch every day. Her name was Roberta. From what I knew, she worked in a notary's office. She'd arrive with a couple coworkers and always ordered a light dish. Even though she was a little too young for my taste, I was struck by her shyness. When I made the rounds of the tables, I exchanged witty remarks with the customers. With women I overdid the compliments, like the lawyer taught me. She lowered her eyes every time, and an embarrassed smile would be sketched on her pretty mouth. Watching her I convinced myself she was submissive by temperament, and it wouldn't be necessary to force her into that role. Physically she attracted me. Tall, slim, built. She didn't have a big chest, but she had one, as well as a cute little ass. Her chestnut hair fell to her shoulders and framed a charming face with well-shaped features. But her legs were nothing to brag about. I took a good look as she crossed them. I noticed her calves weren't thin, and her thighs were traced with cellulite. Imperfections that certainly made her vulnerable and in need of approval. I started to make a play for her. Looks, smiles, little courtesies. I knew nothing about her. I asked Nicoletta, my ex, the dealer of fake Chanel, to poke around. I learned she broke off a six-year relationship with a guy who didn't want to take her to the altar. She lived alone in a small apartment in the suburbs.

"She isn't the right woman for you," my spy remarked.

"Jealous?"

She shook her head. "Roberta's an old-fashioned girl. Marriage, kids, Christmas tree . . . "

I smiled, satisfied. "That's just the kind of woman I want."

Nicoletta gave me a pat on the cheek. "Good luck to you then."

The opportunity to hook up was a headache. One day she came to the bar and asked me for a pill.

I looked in a drawer. "I have some aspirin."

"No, grazie, I'm allergic."

"I had an aunt with the same problem. I remember she'd have to be very careful. Wait, I'll ask the cook. He suffers from migraines and always has a supply of painkillers."

I came back from the kitchen with a tablet. "He told me this should do the trick."

She checked the name of the drug. "It's perfect. Grazie."

"Wednesday is the day we close. Would you like to come out with me?"

She stared at me. "To go where?" she asked, cautious.

"A movie and pizza?"

She pretended to think it over. "OK."

The film was a sugary mishmash with Richard Gere. His girl dies during an operation, and he becomes a better man. I never saw such a boring movie, but Roberta wept the whole time and was wild about it.

"Bellissimo. A great love story. Did you like it?"

"Very much."

At the pizzeria I exploited her state of mind by reeling off a story that was made to order. "I'm a man who's made mistakes for a good part of his life," I began. "Now I'm trying to mend my ways and make up for the bad I've done. Particularly to my family. My father and mother died of heartbreak. My sisters live far away, and I don't have the courage to see them again."

She placed her hand on mine. I told her how wicked teachers and the dark forces of subversion had led astray my young mind. Paris. Central America. The return to Italy. Jail. An incoherent heap of lies, supported only by the shattered tone of my voice.

"This is the first time I've confided in someone," I said at the end.

"I'm pleased you chose me. I heard something about your past, but I didn't imagine you had suffered so much."

She in turn felt the need to confide in me. She spoke of work, her family and especially Alfio. He'd been the love of her life. But when the moment arrived to face up to the subject of marriage, that life slipped away. She had trouble coming back, and now she wasn't sure she wanted to take a chance on another man. I acted as if I understood and tried to reassure her with banal speeches about the sincerity of feelings. Finally I sent her a clear message, revealing my dreams and my plans to her. She seemed the image of my ideal woman. I escorted her to the door of her building, saying goodbye with a chaste kiss on the cheek. As always, she smiled with embarrassment and lowered her eyes.

From that day on we went out every Wednesday. The first month only movies, plays and restaurants. Then one night she came to my house. After dinner I pinned her down on the couch and kissed her. She let me caress her breast, but when I undid the button on her trousers, she said it seemed too soon. While she was putting on her overcoat, I decided to take a chance. The moment had arrived to check whether I made the right choice.

"You'll lose me like this. Forever," I said, my voice a thread.

She stopped in her tracks, petrified. Then she removed her coat and returned to the couch.

"Put on some music. Please."

I didn't have much at home. Some cheap CD's I bought at the supermarket. Reissues of old records, mostly. Music I'd listened to when I went to Saturday afternoon parties and danced the slow numbers with the girls from my school, trying to touch their tits. I put on the first one I grabbed. Caterina Caselli's hits.

Roberta was a terrible lover. The only thing she knew how to do was spread her legs. Despite my desire to go all the way, I conducted myself like a true gentleman, lavishing attention on her. I listened to nine cuts before making her come. She let loose the first squeal as Caselli sang, "Arrivederci amore, ciao, the clouds are already passing." When I got up to throw away the condom, she asked me to replay it.

"It's called 'I'll Never See You Again.'"

"I know. It's sad, but I've always liked it so much."

I pleased her. Amid the sentimental lovers' patter it became "our" song. I used it as a signal when I wanted to take her to bed. Which didn't happen often. I really didn't know what to do with a woman who had no intention of giving me head or letting me fuck her in the ass. But she had many other qualities, and since I wanted to marry her, I didn't make myself sick over it. She was sweet, thoughtful, and didn't break my balls. And at home she kept busy. I loved her company. She filled a hole in my life. At night. In my spare time. With a partner things were more fun. I finally understood why people got married and didn't waste time talking about it. To crown her soap-opera dreams, I took her to Venezia one Wednesday night. A great restaurant, a turn in a gondola, a serenade. In Piazza San Marco, I put a little box in her hand.

"Will you marry me?" I asked at the exact moment when she found herself staring at a ring worth seven grand. Obviously I hadn't paid that price, but that's what it cost.

Roberta was so happy she burst into tears. She hugged me and covered me with kisses. That night I held a passionate woman in my arms, and I understood she needed only to be reassured about my real intentions. She wanted to be certain she'd get to the altar. We decided to set the date after the rehabilitation. We celebrated the engagement at La Nena. Brianese raised his glass and toasted our happiness.

From that moment I began to visit my fiancée's family. And her friends. We often went out with another couple. Luciano and Martina. One glance was enough to tell me she wasn't like my Roberta. Occasionally my eyes met hers, and I got a come-hither look. Her flabby, disagreeable guy more than justified all the heat. None of this escaped my fiancée. Once we got home we had our first quarrel. I wanted to hit her to make her shut up. Instead I just calmed her down. She was one of those women who devote themselves body and soul to a man, but can't take the stress of insecurity. I went on the offensive and did everything I could to make her believe she was the most important person in my life. Making her happy really wasn't so complicated. What she wanted was so predictable. All I needed to do was pay her a little attention. Every so often I surprised her. With luxury. When I closed a deal or my share of the loans arrived, I'd give her some expensive gifts. Like a grande dame. She didn't know I was rich and thought these things might've cost me a lot of sweat.

When she calmed down, I went to bed with Martina. Real sex, finally. But I paid dearly for it. She confided our little escapade to a girlfriend, and the news traveled from mouth to mouth till it reached Roberta's ears. I denied it and held my ground. In the end, she pretended she believed me, but her trust had crumbled. Soon I discovered I was being kept under surveillance. My fiancée was rummaging through my pockets, my wallet, checking the calls on my cell phone, searching for traces of other women. I acted as if nothing was happening. In future I'd have to be more careful.

Sante Brianese called me into his office. The petition for rehabilitation had been filed. The surveillance judge had requested the police to provide reports on my conduct as well as my assets and liabilities.

"I have already moved my pawns," he said. "We have nothing to worry about."

As usual he was right. The reports were all positive. The judge set the hearing for the following month. Thirty days separated me from my new life. Then I could vote, do a thousand other things and especially get rid of that fear of being stopped at a road block. I suggested to Roberta we get married immediately after. Just enough time to arrange for a dream ceremony. She'd already been thinking about it and showed she had some very clear ideas. For the honeymoon too. The Maldives. It didn't seem like such a great place to me, but I wasn't about to object. The preparations would keep her busy, stop her from being eaten up by the suspicion I betrayed her with Martina.

For the first time in a long while I felt really good. Untouchable. The past would never again represent a threat.

ROBERTA

I FELT TOO SECURE. And that was an inexcusable mistake. You can feel secure only when you've never done anything outside the rules. All a guy like me could do was rely on the odds. At the most I could say I felt "reasonably" secure. That was the only way you stopped yourself from lowering your guard. But a mistake I made in the past—and I made lots of them—came back and caught me with my pants down. Anedda. I looked up and found him in front of me. The first thing that crossed my mind was I should've killed him to stop him from coming back into my life. He sure wasn't paying me some courtesy visit. Ferruccio the bull was in a jam. A big jam. You just had to look at him to see he was desperate. Suit wrinkled, face unshaven, eyes glassy and feverish, hair mussed. Before me stood the ghost of the man I once knew. His look said I was his last hope. I poured him a brandy. Cheap stuff. What I used for a caffè corretto. He knocked it back.

"I got to talk to you." He was hoarse. The tension between us was almost as thick as the smoke from his cigarette.

"I have nothing to say to you."

"I'll see you tonight at your place."

"We're not understanding one another."

"*You* don't understand," he hissed. His cockiness was back. "Do what I tell you and don't give me any shit."

As he walked out, I stared at his back, full of hate. I surveyed the customers to see if anybody caught our testy exchange. Everything looked calm. I poured myself two fingers of Lagavullin. The heat of the whiskey wiped out the chill that gripped my gut—for a moment. I too felt desperate. You could bet he wanted to get me involved in some nasty business that'd jeopardize everything I built. Eighteen more days till the hearing for the rehabilitation. I didn't deserve this insult from fate.

I lowered the shutter of the osteria and headed home. The cop didn't ask me for the address. He must've already gotten the lowdown on me. As I was opening the gate, I saw Anedda from the corner of my eye, getting out of an Alfa Romeo black as night. He followed me without a word. Threw himself on a couch.

"I'm bushed," he whined.

He took a cigarette from a pack as wrinkled as his suit.

"What do you want?"

He got right to the point. "You have to ice some dude."

"Forget about it," I shot back. "I'm not killing anybody for you. I've gone straight."

"I know. You've become a regular guy. But if you don't do me this favor, I'm in deep shit. And to limit the damage I'll be forced to cooperate. I'll drag you down with me."

Smart cop. He had me by the balls. I poured myself a drink. "Who am I supposed to kill?"

"An informer of mine. A shitty Algerian who infiltrated the Islamic Salvation Front. We did a couple jobs together. Then he disappeared. I heard he started working for the carabinieri. If I don't shut him up right away, he'll fuck me big time. The carabinieri always manage to make you spill everything."

"Where is he?"

"In Bologna. I spent three days and nights tracking down his hideout. I moved mountains."

"Why don't *you* do this job?"

He burst out laughing. "I'd be happy to do it. But when that asshole goes to a better life, I'll be at my office in Milano. I need an airtight alibi."

"Then you're already under suspicion?"

"Yeah. But they still don't have anything definite on me. They're investigating because I was the Algerian's contact."

"What happened?"

"Nothing that concerns you."

"I won't risk a life sentence in the dark. I want to know about the jam you're in."

"A courier on his way from Iran. A briefcase filled with dollars. You need to know more?"

I shook my head. "How should he die?"

"A bullet in the head. You still have that .22 with the silencer?"

"I've gone straight. I don't need guns anymore."

"Then I'll get you one."

"When do I lay him out?"

"Day after tomorrow. I hope it isn't already too late."

"And after?"

"After what?"

"Are you going to turn up every time you're in deep shit and need somebody whacked?"

"Relax. Once the problem is solved, you'll never see me again."

Right then I knew Anedda wanted to eliminate me as well. Otherwise he would've gotten snotty to remind me I was on-call for him. The business with the Algerian taught him a lesson. No witnesses, no risks.

I heard the key turn in the lock. Roberta. As far as I knew, she should've been at her parents' that night. She rushed into the living room.

"Amore, I have a surprise!" she said, pleased. "A CD with Alessandro Haber singing 'I'll Never See You Again.'"

When she realized she was in the presence of somebody she

didn't know, she immediately buttoned up. "Excuse me," she grumbled, embarrassed. "I thought Giorgio was alone."

The cop got to his feet. "I was about to leave," he said with a forced smile.

"I'll see you out."

"I notice you've stopped going with professionals," he remarked under his breath.

"I've gone straight," I told him for the zillionth time.

"Tomorrow morning I'll drop by the osteria," Anedda promised.

As I closed the door, I muttered a curse.

"Who is he?" asked my fiancée.

I shrugged. "A wine dealer." I cut it short.

"What did he want?"

"He made me an offer."

"Why here at home? They usually go to the osteria."

Roberta was asking too many questions. I hugged her. "I can't wait to hear Haber's version."

She smiled, happy, forgetting about her curiosity. A few seconds later the room filled with the warm voice of the actor who let himself be tempted by music. That night she was the one who wanted to make love. It was the farthest thing from my mind.

"Some other time," I said. My tone was snippy. Her presence rubbed me the wrong way. I needed to be alone to think. In the next twenty-four hours I'd have to kill a man and try not to get myself killed.

I couldn't sleep. Roberta slept calmly at my side, her hand resting on my chest. The problem wasn't murdering the Algerian, but stopping Ferruccio the bull from eliminating me. He had to have a plan already. He wouldn't try anything the day the Algerian died. The need for an alibi forced him to stay put at police headquarters. For several days. Till he'd shaken off the suspicion of being a corrupt cop. After he waited a bit, one night he'd shoot me right in front of my house. Or he'd invite himself over for a drink. More likely. Then he'd have to get rid of Roberta as well. She got a good look at his face. In my company. I wasn't afraid. But I was racked by the unpredictability of fate. I couldn't bear the idea of a life at the mercy of events. If I got through this business, what else was waiting for me? A tumor? A car crash? Brianese's arrest? My heart was pounding, and I had to get up. What the fuck was happening to me? I went into the living room and made myself watch TV. A movie with Franco Franchi. He was playing the part of a monk who went to visit his aunt, the manager of a brothel. After a little while I felt my heartbeat return to normal. I went back to the bedroom to see if my fiancée was sleeping. Then with a screwdriver I pried loose a piece of the baseboard from the wall in the hallway. A recess dug into the wall hid a nylon pouch. I lied to Anedda. I saved the pistol. You never know what might happen. And I made the right decision. The Ruger .22 I used to kill Ausonio and Ciccio Formaggio was dismantled. I'd wrapped the various parts in rags soaked in oil. Barrel, spring, chamber, stock, clip. I screwed on the silencer. Released the firing pin. I was ready to defend my life the only way I knew how. I went back to bed. Roberta squeezed up against me.

The cop showed up after noon. He ordered a coffee. "Tonight I'll drop by your place. I'll bring you the guy's photo and the piece."

"No," I answered, prepared. "My girl will be there. Let's meet at the parking lot behind the bus station."

He mulled over the change in plans for a few seconds. "OK. One-thirty. Sharp."

March had just begun, and the nights were still bitter cold. I slipped on a dark jacket and a warm wool cap. Gifts from my fiancée. The leather gloves I'd bought just that afternoon. I took my bicycle from the storeroom and headed for the meeting. It was a Bianchi from the '50s, repaired and repainted. It cost an arm and a leg, but I couldn't resist because it was identical to my grandfather's. When I was little and went to see him, he'd sit me on the crossbar and take me around town. I used it every day to tool around the centro, now closed to traffic. The parking lot really wasn't deserted. It was scattered with parked cars where Nigerian and Albanian whores took their johns. The black Alfa Romeo was smack in the center of the open space. Ferruccio the bull wanted to be sure he could see who was coming. I stopped at the passenger side. He signaled me to get in. With my foot I lowered the Bianchi's kickstand and opened the door just enough to slip the pistol inside. I pulled the trigger ten times. Every bullet in the clip. The silencer muffled the noise from the shots and smothered the bursts of flame that accompanied each discharge. Sure, people in the parking lot might've noticed that long series of flashes in the darkness, like a strobe light. But they saw and heard absolutely nothing. The shit was dead. Head leaning against the wheel. Eyes wide-open. A trickle of blood dripping from his mouth. I carefully closed the door, climbed on the bike and rode off, pedaling at an easy pace. I got rid of the gloves and the gun, tossing them into a trash can. I was sorry to say goodbye to the Ruger. It had served me faithfully, but at this point it was too hot. The bullets and casings were back in Anedda's body and car. Keeping the gun would be suicide. I was content. But not calm. To take him by surprise I had to give up a safer plan. I would've preferred to lure him to a quiet place, out in the country, so I could torch his car and corpse. But he was too sharp to fall for a trap that obvious. When his body was discovered, the investigators would find the stuff he was going to hand over to me. The gun and the photo of the Algerian. The danger: something might tie me to him. A note. An address. A phone number. A wise precaution would've been to make myself scarce for a while. But I couldn't do that. I'd have to come up with too many explanations for too many people. All I could do was wait. And risk being arrested.

I found Roberta at home. She was waiting for me, reading in an armchair.

"Where have you been?"

"I had a drink with Brianese at another club."

"Did you talk about the hearing?"

"Yeah. Not much time now."

"You weren't with another woman, were you?"

"Please, amore, don't start again."

She threw the home-decorating magazine on the table and opened her arms to welcome me. "Come here."

I let her cuddle me. I needed to relax. I closed my eyes and again saw the scene of Anedda's death. Killing him was necessary. And satisfying. I always liked murder. Ever since the time I shot my friend Luca in the head in that fucking Central American jungle. I also wanted to shoot the bull in the head. And not use the whole clip. I had to do it for fear of missing vital organs. Wounded, even if seriously, he could still draw his nine caliber and pay me back in kind. The investigators would certainly think the killer was unskilled and in a rush. I would've liked them to come upon the work of a pro. A shot in the head is solemn, like a court verdict. It's justice.

Two days later articles about the discovery of Anedda's corpse appeared in the newspapers. Everybody in town was talking about it. The national TV channels arrived in troupes. The journalists speculated about international terrorism. But the media's interest in keeping the story alive didn't match the investigators'. The cops and judges knew very well they weren't dealing with a state servant who sacrificed himself in the line of duty. And they didn't have a single shred of evidence pinpointing a murderer. The people who usually hung around the area didn't mention anything out of the ordinary. The attention to the case lasted a couple days, then vanished, swept away by other events. My tension also vanished. I convinced myself the investigation wouldn't turn up anything related to me. My plan worked.

That night I returned home a little later. I noticed Roberta's bag next to the phone. An unexpected visit. She'd come down with the flu and preferred to stay at her parents'. I found her in the living room. In the dark.

"Do you feel bad, amore?" I asked thoughtfully.

She didn't answer. I switched on the light. Her eyes were puffy from crying. In her hand was a copy of the town daily. She held it up so I could see Anedda's photo. My whole world came crashing down on me. Fate continued to torment me. First Ferruccio the bull. Now my fiancée, suddenly transformed into another dangerous threat.

"It's the man I found in this room a week ago," she said in an accusatory tone.

"You're mistaken. Newspaper photos are deceiving."

"On television I saw some film clips. It's really him. And the night he was killed you weren't home."

"You're accusing me of the crime?" I asked, as if unwilling to believe it.

She started to sob. "I don't know what to think. I'm certain I met this person here."

I acted indignant. "I already told you it wasn't him. Besides, I was with Brianese when they shot him. If you don't believe me, ask him."

I knew she wouldn't dare approach the lawyer to ask him a question like that. My answer should've calmed her down. But she was still ripped by doubt.

I hugged her. "How can you think I'm a murderer? Do you want me to die of grief?"

She squeezed me tight. "I can't believe you're a monster. But you knew that policeman, and you have a duty to report what you know to the investigators."

The blood froze in my veins. The thing was getting worse. I had to cook up something else. Otherwise she'd go to the cops and tell them she saw Anedda at my house forty-eight hours before he was whacked.

I took her face in my hands. "Yeah, I knew him," I admitted. "I was one of his informers. The terrorists are reorganizing, and my experience proved useful to him. I didn't tell you before because it involves tricky, secret investigations. But I'm not the one who killed him. Get it into your head once and for all."

"One more reason to clear yourself," she stubbornly insisted. "Your information can help to capture the murderer and his accomplices."

"I can't believe that'll happen. But even if it did, it would mean blowing my cover, turning myself into a target. I'd have to go into hiding, leave my job, give up the idea of living with you."

This argument threw her civic sense into crisis. Now was the time to lay it on thick. "In a few days I'll have the chance to remove the stigma of being an ex-convict. A new life awaits me. A life with you. If I go to the police, the petition process will be suspended, and who knows how long I'll have to wait. Don't force me to give you up. I want to marry you. And I want a child."

My soap-opera performance worked. Roberta wept buckets, letting go of every doubt. I picked up Caterina Caselli's CD. Played "I'll Never See You Again." Then I took her in my arms and carried her to bed. Whispered sweet words of love. When she fell asleep, I sighed with relief. For the moment I was out of danger. But in future? Taken by surprise, I slipped her the wrong lie. I should've told her I already spoke to the investigators, maintaining my cover as an informer. Too late now to put it right. My only hope was marriage. To tie her to me with a knot that can't be untied. Till that moment I'd been firmly opposed to the religious ritual. As soon as she awoke, I'd tell her I changed my mind and we'd get married in her parish church. And we wouldn't miss a single class in the prenuptial course. Ours will be a blessed union. Absolved from every sin.

It was a winning move. My fiancée relaxed and didn't mention the topic of Anedda again. She went back to busying herself with the preparations for the wedding. And I made the acquaintance of her confessor, Don Agostino, who was going to guide us on the path to the sacrament of matrimony. An old priest, sour and pigheaded. The loathing was mutual from the first time we met. But I was ready to put up with anything just to lead her to the altar. The day of the hearing for the rehabilitation arrived. The surveillance judge read out a long report. He asked me several questions. Then he gave the word to the public prosecutor.

"I do not object to granting the benefit." He said no more.

Brianese spoke for five minutes. He described my wish for reinstatement in calm, effective language.

"How did it go?" Roberta asked the lawyer when we left the courtroom.

"Fine. Now it's just a matter of waiting for the decision. As Giorgio probably explained to you, the court of surveillance will communicate it in writing. You'll have to be patient a few more days."

We celebrated at La Nena after closing. Because it was convenient. Ten or so friends and the lawyer. Champagne, terrines of foie gras, a torta. Sante Brianese began amusing us with courtroom anecdotes. Suddenly I heard Roberta's voice asking, "What are they saying about the policeman killed in the parking lot?"

The lawyer shrugged. "Next to nothing. The anti-terrorist squad is investigating, and their lips are sealed. To tell the truth, it's a case I haven't followed much. The day of the murder I was in Roma for a suit in appellate court, and when I returned, there was no longer any talk of it."

Fucked. That's just how I felt then. I was celebrating the rehabilitation, and my fiancée was digging my grave with her fucking questions. Roberta was pale; she stared at me, confused. She remained in this condition till the party ended. We went home without saying a word to one another. She locked herself in the bathroom and cried. For the second time in a few days I sank into a state of absolute desperation. When she calmed down, she'd expect some answers. And there wasn't a lie in the world that could get me out of this mess. I could only hope to cut my losses.

All of a sudden I found myself in front of her. Her face streaked with mascara. "Where did you go that night?"

"Brianese is mistaken. He always has too much going on. He got confused."

"Where did you go?" she shouted.

"Maybe I'm the one who's mistaken. I really don't remember. I may have taken a walk."

"Where?" She screamed so loud she turned red in the face.

I had one last move to shake off her suspicions. "OK. You asked for it." I screamed back. "I was with another woman."

"You bastard." She attacked me, trying to hit me in the face. "You went to bed with that whore Martina, didn't you?"

"No. I picked up some woman on the street." I hugged her close. "It was just a fuck. You're the one I love."

She got free and ran to lock herself in the bathroom. Ten minutes later she opened the door. She had washed her face and combed her hair.

"I don't want to marry you anymore."

"What are you saying?"

"I thought you were a different person. But you're just a liar."

"You're upset now. You have reason to be, but this isn't the time to make decisions that can jeopardize our future."

She left without listening. I collapsed on the couch. I felt like hitting the bottle of whiskey, but I needed a clear head. Losing Roberta was no big deal. That was sure as shit. Our relationship was hanging by a thread, and to go through with the wedding plans would be plain stupid. I'd start circulating some not-very-flattering rumors about her. After a while the gossip about our break-up would die down. Replacing her wouldn't be hard. The real problem was different. Would she keep her mouth shut about Anedda's murder or blab about it to her mother, her girlfriends and Don Agostino? The answer was obvious. She'll have to go into detail about why she called off the wedding, and you can bet she'll tell how she made me confess my betrayal. Then the meeting with Anedda at my place will pop out. Somebody'll persuade her to talk to the cops. But she won't even need to put the police on my trail. A story like that could generate all kinds of rumors—which will eventually reach the wrong ears. Even if Anedda was a corrupt cop, his colleagues were still keen to find who filled him with lead.

I weighed the idea of clearing out. I was sitting on a nest egg that'd take me a long ways away. But I shouldn't have to start all over again. It wasn't right. Suddenly it dawned on me: I had to kill Roberta. I didn't want to go that far, but the rule "no witness, no risk" stood out crystal-clear. Still, it was just as clear I was dealing with a problem that had no quick fix. If she died violently, suspicion would fall on her fiancé, who was just rehabilitated but nonetheless had a shady past. She was a nice girl, conscientious about her job, with a deeply religious outlook on life. In her world, murder wasn't considered a likely event. No, it was so unusual the police would be obliged to carry out a serious investigation. If it was a question of a hooker, a junkie, a vagrant, an illegal immigrant or simply a woman connected to some marginal character, the news of the murder would take up a paragraph in the dailies and half a page of a police report. I sized up various possibilities. The most convincing was passing off the crime as the work of a maniac. But in the end the cops would still come knocking at my door. No matter how I looked at it, I remained the principal suspect. I closed my eyes. Thought about her from the first time I spotted her in the osteria. The memory of a conversation made something click in my mind. At first I didn't know what. The more I thought about it, the more precise it grew, and an idea took shape. Then a plan.

I woke up earlier than usual. I waited for Don Agostino to finish saying the seven o'clock mass. I caught up with him on his way to the rectory, followed by two altar-boys.

"I need to talk to you. It's important."

"I don't have time this morning," he answered rudely.

"Something serious has happened between me and Roberta. Give me a few minutes. Please."

He raised his eyes towards the sky. "Wait for me in my office. I'll be with you after I change."

It took him a good half an hour to show up. From the bread crumbs on his cassock I figured he spent it having breakfast.

"Now tell me what happened."

"Padre, I did a very bad thing. I cheated on Roberta," I said immediately to attract his attention. I wanted him to remember every word of that conversation. "One night I couldn't resist temptation, so I bought the body of a prostitute. I realized I erred when I found my fiancée waiting for me. In the beginning I didn't have the courage to confess what I did, so I lied to justify going out that night. Then, through a series of events, my lie was discovered, and I was forced to tell the truth."

"Lies have short legs," he remarked, satisfied. "What do you want from me?"

"Roberta doesn't want to marry me anymore. You must persuade her to reconsider her decision. She won't talk to me."

"Perhaps you are not the right man for her. Her parents have always been convinced of it. In the past you were guilty of grave offenses, and even now, a few months before your marriage, your conduct continues to be immoral."

"It was a moment of weakness. It will never happen again. I am deeply in love with Roberta. I'm certain I can make her happy."

"I shall try to speak to her. But I promise you nothing. To lie and to go with prostitutes are grave sins. That girl does not deserve such pain."

I put on a contrite expression and left in silence.

My second stop was a local library. At that hour of the morning it was filled mostly with pensioners. I found the book I wanted. Verified the accuracy of my memories and left for work. The day passed without a hitch. A customer came to ask me for a loan. Two and a half grand. He'd pay me back three the following week. I gave him what he wanted. Sometimes regulars would ask me for small amounts in cash. Till then I'd send them to one of the loansharks I did business with. But after giving it some thought I decided I could set up a little bank in the osteria. The secret to preventing the cops from nosing around was to limit yourself to low figures. All through the day I acted happy. Talked to various people about the wedding, asked their advice about flowers and photographs. Shortly before closing I received a phone call from Roberta.

"I have to talk to you."

"Don Agostino?"

"Yes, he convinced me. We must look into the depths of our hearts and determine the sincerity of our feelings."

"I'll wait for you at home."

Her face looked wasted. She seemed worn-out. She sat in the armchair.

"It hurts me to see you suffer like this."

"It's your fault."

"What have your mother and your friends been telling you?" I asked to get the lie of the land.

She shook her head. "I haven't said anything yet. I'm too ashamed to say what you've done."

"You did right not to tell anybody about it. I'm certain we'll be able to reach an understanding. And everything will go back to what it was before."

From her bag she took out a handkerchief and started to whimper. "I don't trust you anymore."

"Please, don't cry. It'll be hard to talk."

She dried her eyes and blew her nose. "I've never felt so bad in my entire life."

I caressed her cheek. "Have you had dinner?"

She shook her head. "I can't get anything down."

"You'll make yourself sick." I raised my voice, worried.

"I'll eat something at home."

"I've brought a couple orders of cannelloni with ricotta from the osteria. I was just about to sit down and eat. Come on, keep me company."

I added another plate. Offered her a glass of wine while the meal was heating up in the microwave. I let her serve herself. She took only one of the cannelloni. I passed her the grated cheese. We ate in silence.

"Don Agostino thinks you're not suited to marriage. He's convinced you're an amoral person."

"He's wrong."

"Then why did you go with that prostitute?"

"It's your fault. Sexually you leave a lot to be desired."

She blushed with shame. "I need time. You have much more experience, and besides, I don't like some of the things you want to do with me. They seem dirty, unnatural between two people who want to marry."

"Is that your opinion or Don Agostino's?"

"He's my confessor."

"But he has no experience in this area. And he's giving you bad advice. For example, what do you think about when you touch yourself?"

"Stop it. I don't want to talk about these things."

"You should've taken your fantasies to bed, not to the confessional. We would've enjoyed ourselves, and I wouldn't have felt the need to drill a prostitute."

"Don't use language like that. It's disgusting."

"Why did Alfio leave you?"

"That's none of your business."

"You couldn't satisfy him. That's the truth. He broke the engagement. I went looking for pleasure elsewhere. What do you think the next guy will do?"

She burst into tears. I decided to tone down the discussion. By now she had to be convinced I went out that night to satisfy the needs of the flesh.

I hugged her tight. "I love you, Roberta. I don't want to lose you. I swear on the memory of my father and mother I'll never go with another woman again. I'll make love only to you. Without forcing you. And with respect for your sensitivity."

She took my face in her hands and looked me straight in the eyes. "Do you really swear it?"

"I swear it. Don Agostino made me realize sex is only one aspect of a couple's life."

"How I'd like to believe you."

"Do it, and you'll be happy."

"I'm confused. First the story about the murdered policeman. Then the humiliation of being betrayed with a common whore."

"Don't think about it anymore. Think of our future."

"I can't," she came right back, depressed. "Was she prettier than me?"

I smiled. "That would be impossible."

"Was she black?"

"No."

"Did you kiss her on the mouth?"

"No."

"Did you use a condom?"

"Yes."

"I want to know what you did."

"Enough now. That would be humiliating for both of us."

A tense silence fell on the scene. I let her chill a bit. Offered her a cigarette and a liqueur. Switched on the TV. Tuned in that comic news program, *Striscia la Notizia*. Gabibbo, the life-size puppet, put her in a good mood. I suggested she have a slice of tiramisù. It was her favorite dessert. And the cook at La Nena did an excellent version of it.

"Are you trying to ply me with sweets?" she joked.

"With everything. Just to win back your heart."

She ate two slices. Washed them down with some aged Marsala. Then she stood up. "I'm going home."

"Stay here, please. Being together will help us get back on track."

"OK. Besides, I'm too tired to drive home."

When she woke up, I brought her breakfast in bed. Latte macchiato and some store-bought cookies.

"I want to treat you like a princess."

She smiled at me. "I have to hurry. Otherwise I'll be late for work."

"I'll expect you for lunch."

At the osteria I served her linguine al pesto. With lots of parmigiano. Her mood had improved. Even if she still felt tired. And annoyed by a persistent itch on her face and hands.

"Your body is reacting to the stress of these past few days," I remarked. "It'll pass soon."

When she came back that evening, the itch was worse. It spread to her chest and groin.

"Go to my place. I'll get there as soon as I can. And don't eat too much. Maybe it's an infection. There's some yogurt in the fridge."

I waited about an hour. Then I told the waiters I was worried about my fiancée, she wasn't feeling well. I asked the oldest guy to take care of the closing that night.

When I entered the house, I noticed the yogurt container on the edge of the armchair. I picked it up. It was empty. I went into the bedroom. Roberta was lying in bed. In a nightgown. Motionless. Her face transfigured by the pink wheals of a serious skin eruption.

"I feel sick. Call a doctor."

"That doesn't seem necessary," I said.

She touched her face. "Oh God," she moaned. "What's happening to me?"

I sat on the edge of the bed. "You're dying, Roberta. You've swallowed an excessive quantity of aspirin. And you know that acetylsalicylic acid may be harmful to your health."

"What are you saying?"

"I put crushed aspirins in all the food you've eaten in the last twenty-four hours," I explained as I slipped into her bag the box of aspirin I used. "In the cannelloni, the milk, the parmigiano—"

"You've poisoned me."

"Yes. I remembered you once told me you were allergic to aspirin. I had an aunt with the same problem. The thing struck me because, at the time, I couldn't believe a medicine might kill a person."

"Call a doctor, I beg you."

"It isn't necessary. My diagnosis is correct."

"Why are you killing me?"

"I can't let you go around telling people you met Anedda here. Not even that I went out for a walk the night he was murdered."

"It was you?"

"Yes. Don't ask me why. Pray instead. From what I could verify today at the library, according to the international medical literature, you should pop off in a couple hours at the most."

She grabbed her throat. "Help, I can't breathe."

"It's the respiratory attack. You're on your way out, bella mia."

Roberta fought for life tooth and nail. She started to curse me. Her voice had become hoarse. And unbearable. I went into the living room and switched on the stereo. Caterina Caselli's voice filled the house.

You need to have a heart so pure
To see the heaven that's hidden here
You need to love, be ever so sure,
To banish every fear

Roberta, in the meantime, had turned cyanotic. Blue lips and nails. From the way her lips were moving, I could tell she was remanding her soul to the Lord. I looked at the clock. She could die of respiratory insufficiency or cardiovascular collapse. The important thing was that she be quick about it. As soon as she lost consciousness, I called the ambulance. And put on my pajamas.

"I woke up and found her like this."

When they loaded her on the stretcher, she was still alive. But she wouldn't make it. Too late. I sighed with relief. I was fed up with playing the role of sweetheart. All that soap-opera mush I'd been forced to say turned my stomach.

The autopsy revealed the cause of death. Respiratory insufficiency. The toxicological tests isolated the substance that produced it. The parents maintained that never ever would their Roberta have taken acetylsalicylic acid. They were so convincing a couple carabinieri in plain clothes showed up at my house. The osteria was closed for mourning.

I played the role of the shattered man. I didn't manage to impress them.

"Were you aware of the fact that your fiancée was allergic to aspirin?" asked the marshal.

"No, I didn't know."

"How was that possible?" asked the sergeant.

"How was what possible?"

"That you didn't know," explained his partner.

"She never told me."

"The medical examiner told us it would take quite a bit to die. How can it be that you noticed nothing?"

"Roberta came to the restaurant. She said she didn't feel well—"

"We know all about this. We talked to the staff. We asked you a different question."

"When I came home, Roberta was in bed. She was sleeping."

"She wasn't sleeping. She was dying—"

"She seemed to be sleeping. I put on my pajamas and got into bed."

"And you noticed nothing."

"No."

"You didn't even kiss her good night?"

"No."

"That's strange. Fiancés and newlyweds always kiss good night."

"That night we didn't."

"How did you notice your fiancée was sick?"

"I had to go to the bathroom. I switched on the light. I saw Roberta's face was swollen and her lips were purple. I immediately called the ambulance."

"But when you got into bed, you didn't notice her face was swollen?"

"No. She was turned on her side."

They remained silent for a little while, staring at me, perplexed.

"Were you getting on well together?" asked the marshal.

"Recently there were some differences. But everything had been settled."

"What was the nature of these 'differences'?"

"I don't think they'll interest you."

"But they do interest us."

"Don't play asshole, Pellegrini," the sergeant intervened. "Even if they're cleaning up your record, you're still a criminal to us. And we beat the fuck out of criminals."

"Do what you want."

"Don Agostino told us a juicy little tale."

"OK, so I've been with a whore."

"Do you remember which one?"

"No."

"Do you at least remember where?"

"The highway near the industrial zone."

"What day was it?"

I shrugged. "I don't remember. What does it matter anyway?"

"We're paid to ask the questions. Even the ones that don't matter."

"You want to hear a question that matters?"

I spread my arms. "Let me hear it."

"Did you give your girl the aspirin?"

"No."

"Then where did she get it?"

"In a pharmacy, I guess."

"Her family says that's impossible. She knew it would kill her."

"Then I don't know."

"In the days before her death, did she talk about having a headache, menstrual cramps, fever or some other ailment?"

"She told me she was bothered by a bad itch."

"Nothing else?"

"Nothing else."

The marshal closed his notebook and headed for the door, promptly aped by his colleague.

He put his hand on the knob, then turned towards me. "Only three theories explain Roberta's death: accident, homicide or suicide. We can easily exclude accident. Either she decided to put an end to the pain and humiliation you caused her or you killed her."

"Why would I kill Roberta? I loved her, I wanted to marry her."

"Right, the motive," he said, thinking. "If it were up to me, I'd throw you in jail till the investigation is over. But no judge would sign an arrest warrant on the basis of suspicion, without a clear motive."

"We'll see you soon," added the sergeant. "Maybe back at the station."

I went to the kitchen to make myself coffee. Lit a cigarette and took my time, enjoying it. The thing went well. The cops had nothing. The inquest would be shelved. Only a question of time. I was dead sure. But just to cover my back I phoned Brianese.

"Don't worry, Giorgio." His tone was sympathetic. "I'll speak to the prosecutor. And I'll ask our friends in uniform to intervene. I guarantee you these two guys won't bother you again."

Yes, our friends. All of them were at the funeral. Even the loansharks. In church only Roberta's parents and relatives didn't deem me worthy of a glance. Somehow they held me responsible for her death. Sante Brianese came to sit at my side.

He squeezed my arm. "The notification from the court of surveillance has arrived. You've been rehabilitated."

I burst into tears. Of happiness. I'd done it. The nightmare was over. I could finally be like everybody else. Just a face in the crowd. I wiped my eyes. I couldn't wait for that torment to end. Somebody squeezed my hand. It was Martina. In her look I read the determination to take Roberta's place. I returned her squeeze. I'd marry her. And I'd never kill anyone else. No need to. I finally managed to cut off every tie with the past. The present and future were represented by a community that had a sense of friendship and solidarity. Plus business sense. I'd be considered a respected and honest citizen, employed only in earning his daily bread. And enjoying his money.

The cemetery was lit by a beautiful warm sun. The mourning procession followed the hearse in absolute silence. You could hear only the noise of steps on the gravel paths.

My wreath was the biggest. On the ribbon I had them write "Arrivederci amore, ciao." A goodbye kiss. I couldn't think of anything else.

Massimo Carlotto was born in Padua, Italy, and now lives in Cagliari, Sardinia. In addition to the many titles in his extremely popular Alligator series, he is also the author of *The Fugitive*, *The Obscure Immensity of Death*, *Niente, più niente al mondo* and most recently, *Northeast*. One of Italy's most popular authors and a major exponent of the Mediterranean Noir novel, Carlotto has been compared with many of the most important American hardboiled crime writers. His novels have been translated into many languages, enjoying enormous success outside of Italy, and several have been made into highly acclaimed films.

AVAILABLE NOW from EUROPA EDITIONS

The Big Question
by Wolf Erlbruch
translated by Michael Reynolds

Best Book at the 2004 Children's Book Fair in Bologna.

A stunningly beautiful and poetic illustrated book for children
that poses the biggest of all big questions: why am I here?
A chorus of voices—including the cat's, the baker's, the pilot's
and the soldier's—offers us some answers. But nothing is certain,
except that as we grow each one of us will pose the question
differently and be privy to different answers.

AVAILABLE NOW from EUROPA EDITIONS

Total Chaos

by Jean-Claude Izzo

translated by Howard Curtis

"Jean-Claude Izzo's […] growing literary renown and huge sales
are leading to a recognizable new trend in continental fiction:
the rise of the sophisticated Mediterranean thriller . . .
Caught between pride and crime, racism and fraternity,
tragedy and light, messy urbanization and generous beauty,
the city for [detective Fabio Montale] is a Utopia, an ultimate port
of call for exiles. There, he is torn between fatalism
and revolt, despair and sensualism." —*The Economist*

This first installment in the legendary Marseilles Trilogy
sees Fabio Montale turning his back on a police force
marred by corruption and racism and taking
the fight against the mafia into his own hands.

AVAILABLE NOW from EUROPA EDITIONS

Hangover Square
by Patrick Hamilton

Adrift in the grimy pubs of London at the outbreak
of World War II, George Harvey Bone is hopelessly infatuated
with Netta, a cold, contemptuous, small-time actress.
George also suffers from occasional blackouts.
During these moments one thing is horribly clear: he mission
is to murder Netta. "Hamilton […] is a sort of urban
Thomas Hardy: […] always a pleasure to read,
and as a social historian he is unparalleled." —Nick Hornby

FORTHCOMING FICTION from EUROPA EDITIONS

I Loved You For Your Voice
by Sélim Nassib

translated by Alison Anderson

Love, desire, and song set against the colorful backdrop
of modern Egypt. The story of the Arab world's greatest
and most popular singer, Om Kalthoum, told through
the eyes of the poet Ahmad Rami, who wrote her lyrics
and loved her in vain all his life. Spanning over five decades
in the history of modern Egypt, this passionate tale of love
and longing provides a key to understanding the soul,
the aspirations and the disappointments of the Arab world.
"A total immersion into the Arab world's magic and charm."
—Avvenimenti

Release date: February, 2006

FORTHCOMING FICTION from EUROPA EDITIONS

Love Burns

by Edna Mazya

translated by Dalya Bilu

Ilan, a middle-aged professor of astrophysics, discovers
that his young wife is having an affair. Terrified of losing her,
he decides to confront her lover instead. Their meeting ends
in the latter's murder—the unlikely murder weapon being
Ilan's pipe—and in desperation, Ilan disposes of the body
in the fresh grave of his kindergarten teacher.
But when the body is discovered . . . "Starts out
as a psychological drama and becomes a strange, funny,
unexpected hybrid: a farce thriller. A great book." —*Ma'ariv*

Release date: March, 2006

FORTHCOMING FICTION from EUROPA EDITIONS

Departure Lounge
by Chad Taylor

Two young women mysteriously disappear. The lives of those
they have left behind—lovers, acquaintances, and strangers
intrigued by their disappearance—intersect to form a captivating
latticework of odd coincidences and surprising twists of fate.
Urban noir at its stylish and intelligent best. "Entropy noir . . .
The hypnotic pull lies in the zigzag dance of its forlorn characters,
casting a murky, uneasy sense of doom." —*The Guardian*

Release date: April, 2006

FORTHCOMING FICTION from EUROPA EDITIONS

The Jasmine Isle

by Ioanna Karystiani

translated by Michael Eleftheriou

A modern love story with the force of an ancient Greek tragedy.
Set on the spectacular Cycladic island of Andros, The Jasmine Isle,
one of the finest literary achievements in contemporary
Greek literature, recounts the story of the old sea wolf,
Spyros Maltambès, and the beautiful Orsa Saltaferos,
sentenced to marry a man she doesn't love and to watch
while the man she does love is wed to another.

Release date: April, 2006